SHULA

with love

I Am Beryl, A Chronology

Book 3

JUSTINE ORME

To SHULA with Love

Cover Photo: shutterstock ID 524284342 by Sundraw Photography

Cover Design: Kyra Matla (Front)
Colleen Kaluza (spine and back)

Editor & Co-Publisher: Colleen Kaluza of www.WordWyze.nz

Photo of Justine Orme: © Colleen Kaluza

Printed in New Zealand by YourBooks.co.nz
A catalogue record for this book is available from the
National Library of New Zealand

Printed Soft-cover Edition: ISBN-13: 978-0-473-66203-5
E-book Edition: ISBN-13: 978-0-473-66204-2

This book is written

for every

SHULA

Find who you

really are

ENDORSEMENTS

Reading 'Shula' has been like watching a rosebud unfold. The Shula I met in chapter 1 is quite different to Yeshua's beloved of the last chapter. Chapter by chapter, she, who was known to Father before her conception, unfolded like a rose, petal by petal. Her personhood grew, her spirit grew, her love for God grew. Shula touched me in many ways. I saw myself in her struggles, in her successes. I was drawn in & inspired to look inwards. I loved the pictures that Justine's words painted. I could see heaven. I could see the spirit beings. I could see what Shula was seeing. I could feel as she did. Best of all, just as Shula was invited into divine intimacy, I too, was invited into the same intimacy. Pure Joy.

Lyn Garrard

Shula is an exquisite love story, written from the Lover to His Beloved. The story, as told thru Beryl's eyes, intricately highlights the struggles and successes of the young believer as she navigates her way through life.
Shula's story shows the way in which the spiritual and physical realms interact on a daily basis, sometimes we recognise it but mostly we do not.
I highly recommend this work of art, it is life-changing and will surely challenge your perspective.

Jenny Smith

ACKNOWLEDGEMENTS

My grateful thanks to the team who surrounded me for nearly two years during this most arduous of writings. Through illness, breakages, what seemed to be crisis after crisis, until I never thought this book would be written.

But you were all there pushing me along to get this finished.

Thank you.

Janet Huddleston; Jenny Smith; Margaret Rose MacDonald; Lyn Garrard; Terry Cochius.

Thank you to Stan – again, Honey - you put up with hours of my absence as I closet myself away in the study, and all you can hear is the keyboard. You bring me cups of tea, keep me fed and then sometimes insist I take a break.

And above all - oh Holy Spirit. THANK YOU. This was marvellous. What truths you revealed. What wonderful things I have seen.

JUSTINE'S FOREWORD

When I started writing Shula, I had thought to follow the Song of Solomon narrative, but wondered how to present the rather graphic aspects of the story.

There were quite a few false starts and then meanwhile, I broke both my wrists, so there was no writing done at all for about six months.

Then, once I was able to write again, it just flowed - not at all how I had envisioned the story.

All I can say, is that Holy Spirit is all over this book, the fingerprints of God marking each passage.

I am excited for you to read it and see what I saw, for as I write, it's not my imagination; I literally see the drama played out in front of me, then it's my job to put words to the movie I am seeing.

Of necessity, this is a love story, for how great is the love of Jesus?

Please, let me know what you think of Shula.

1

Get me a fan. I'm getting all hot and flustered.

I Am Beryl, and I bear witness to the greatest love story ever told, explicit in its passion.

Driven love.

When I, Beryl, was next mentioned in the Holy Writings, it was with shock and awe as I saw how the Most High of All used something that some consider profane and unholy; base even, to show His extraordinary passion and love for man who wanders the earth.

The wisest man who has ever lived, had a play written and in it, he described his love for a girl.

Solomon had MANY girls, 1000 of them in fact, but one appeared to be above all the others: the Shulamite woman.

I tremble as I recall the words used in this opera. Tremble with astonishment and desire. The desire to be consumed by love. He who is love.

That the Most High of All craves the company of mortal man so much, that He painted this allegory using Solomon's love and carnal desires.

The play begins with the Lord God wooing mankind, speaking in a language people can relate to and understand. Oh, how potent is the wine of the wooing:

"I am come into my garden, my sister, my spouse:

I have gathered my myrrh with my spice."

How could the Most High of All use such language? How can He say He has come into our garden? Of course, we know what garden was being spoken about; this is after all a love story.

That God would come to the level of man and talk plainly in language easily understood; surely, He is above the things of the natural way? That the King of all Kings would speak in a way man can relate to – how beautiful!

And you see – He even uses myrrh which is precious.

The Most High of All tells of how He desires to have the relationship of intimacy with man – intimacy of love and romance, passion and desire.

When I understood this, I'm sure my golden radiance glowed even more.

King Solomon used me in his rings -

> *"His hands are as gold rings set with the Beryl; his belly is as bright ivory overlaid with sapphires"*
> *Song of Solomon 5:14*

How extraordinary.

Almighty God reaches out to mankind, and He has adorned His hands with gold, with me, Beryl, reflecting the golden glory that surrounds His people. God the Father entered into this allegory song, declaring His passionate love for mankind.

God, the Father of Love, wrote a book about how much He is in love with man. I, Beryl, play such a small part, but I'm there the whole way through, showing His glory, being reflected in the planes and facets of my face.

The Most High of All is insanely in love with mankind who walks the earth, and He is showing us that through this story.

How can mankind resist such great love? Do you not feel the power and persuasion of the High King calling you? How can you decide to walk away when The Most High of All is pursuing YOU.

Doesn't your heart melt within you, do you feel the flames of love being fanned.

Let the Most High of All pursue you, don't run. Allow yourself the freedom to be overcome with His love and passion, His desire to have you as His child.

He comes to man to anoint him with myrrh – myrrh that is used in the Holy Temple as an incense offering to the Most High of All. Myrrh whose meaning shows us that we are wrapped tightly, enveloped. So, God was showing us how He has wrapped us tightly in His love.

This is truly love.

Let me tell you this story.

2

Yeshua sat at His desk. He picked me up, turning me over so that my facets twinkled and shone, reflecting His image.

He smiled at me. I smiled at Him.

All things are created by the will of the Father and the spoken Word that is the Son, for He is the Word. He placed me on His finger. Instantly I was part of a ring.

He kissed me, leaving His lips imprinted on me. "Now you are the seal of my love, Beryl."

Such honour. A kiss of love. The seal of love from lips that can never lie. The kiss of covenant love. His covenant seal of authority.

"You will bear witness to the foretelling of my heart's desire," He said. "There is a scene being played out among my people, and I need you to chronicle it."

I sang in joy to my Lord, and watched with eagerness as He started to write...

3

Dearest Shula,

When it was your time to leave my Father's heart and go to earth to start your journey, I was there. I heard my Father prophesy over you, and watched the scribes enter those prophesies into your Book of Life. I saw the Angels carry you to your mother's womb.

I was there when you were born. I heard your first cry and saw your tiny fists clenched as you sought to make sense of the large space you had just been thrust into: A precursor for what Father had prophesied over you.

And I loved you then, just as I love you now.

Those times you lay awake and your parents would watch you as your eyes followed me around the room. You could see me, they couldn't. They had long since lost their child-like ability to be able to see me. You would gurgle, talking to me, and I would whisper in love back to you.

Now, beloved Shula, you have grown beyond baby-hood. You have left your childish days behind, and you are now a young woman.

How beautiful you are, my Shula! How I long for you to remember the prophesies on your scroll and dance with me, just as we did before; before you left us to go to earth.

I miss you. And so, to awaken you to my desire for you, I will come to you again, in your dreams, in your thoughts, and speak to you there.

With love always,
Jesus.

Yeshua read again what he had written and smiled, satisfied with the message and then kissing me, pressed me into the sealing wax, permanently embedding his covenant love into the letter.

Such love, imparted from the King of Love to His chosen one. I and all of Heaven were eagerly awaiting Shula's response. Surely no one could resist this wooing?

Let him kiss me
with the kisses
of His mouth,
for your love
is more delightful
than wine.
Song of Solomon 1:2

4

We stood in the Council of the Just. Those who were in the Righteous Government and those whom Yeshua had appointed over the affairs of man, bowed deeply before Him. The Twenty-Four Elders took their place on their thrones.

The Spirit of Holiness pervaded everything. She declared the power of God to all, searching hearts and minds, laying bare all thoughts. All were with one heart, one mind, one purpose. All were here to bring Shula to her beloved, to draw her to him; into her rightful place by His side; His bride.

My fellow stones adorning the Lord's breastplate sang together, remembering all we had witnessed, all the past faithfulness of our Lord.

Yeshua spoke, and Shula's Timeline appeared with the Living Letters weaving in and out of the spoken word.

"Nothing will be left off the completion of her Timeline." And as Yeshua spoke, the Jots and Tittles glowed brighter, joyous in their acknowledgment of His words. The Timeline pulsated with life.

When viewed from differing aspects, Shula's Timeline showed brilliantly where it had begun, and slowly the beauty dulled as her life progressed, until very little light remained. Yeshua touched that portion of it. I was intrigued.

"Shula, I call you back to myself, back to my side. For you are blood bought. I paid the ultimate price for you."

As He spoke, Living Letters rode His breath of life and dove into the Timeline.

The Timeline throbbed with life, glowing even brighter as the Word was spoken and the Living Letters danced their joy. Where there had been any dullness in Shula's life, light started to grow. Yeshua stood for a moment observing. Reaching for a Jot, He moved it into a different position. Indicating to an Angel, He pointed to a place and the Angel instantly became part of Shula's Timeline. Yeshua's hands moved rapidly, repositioning, changing, altering and inserting events, times, places, people whom Shula would meet, who were signposts, all pointing towards Him.

Finally, we stood back and admired the King's handiwork. "Now everything is in place," He said.

"I charge you all to complete this important mission." Yeshua looked at the Angels, the Elders and all others gathered to this crucial meeting.

"I give you my word, Shula. You are mine; I am yours." My Lord knew He was not just speaking His heart, but declaring before all the realms that He is TRUTH.

Truth shot as a flaming arc of light, piercing outer darkness, and Shula's timeline followed through the space created. The Heavens lit up and the Living Letters shouted their names, and all creation, all that belonged to every realm there is, vibrated with Truth.

Shin ש glowed brilliantly, her name spelling the first letter of Shula's name. "To consume, to consume, to consume," she sang declaring her purpose.

"Consumed in Love, consumed in Holiness, consumed in passion. All-consuming fire, all-consuming purpose."

Vav ו took up singing her sound. "I am holding the past to the future, your world to ours, we are securely hooked together. It was, it will be, connected, hooked together. Yeshua is the hook; the past, the present and the future."

"Come towards the King," sang ל Lamed. "Teach your tongue that Yeshua is your teacher, go toward Him. I am the shepherd's crook; I will direct you. Your heart will be taught that Yeshua is the King of all kings, the Almighty." Her beautiful rich contralto tones washed around and lapped at the feet of all.

"To behold the face of Yeshua, to reveal Him to you," ה Heh spoke and if those present were not listening properly, they would have wondered whether she thundered, or sighed as the wind, for the revelation of the Son was both.

And thus, all that had been planned for eons was put into place.

The Lord and I left the Council of the Just and came into His garden, His place of rest. We strolled along the various paths, stopping to talk to the little creatures who ran to Him.

I adored this time. The aroma of the Rose of Sharon both soothed and uplifted. I loved it here. Now, to just wait for all that the Lord had decreed to come to pass. Firstly, He would visit Shula in her dreams. Oh, such wonder, such amazing plan and design.

I am a rose of Sharon,
a lily of the valleys.
Like a lily
among thorns
is my darling
among the maidens.

Song of Solomon 2:1

5

Shula yawned and stretched. The half-remembered dream fleeting too quickly as she woke up from her night's sleep. Yet the essence of it remained in her spirit. It was as though while she slept, longing had taken root in her heart, ousting complacency. She touched her lips. Did they feel different? His kiss lingered, an insubstantial, dream-quality memory. She searched for the fragrance of his perfume, willing the olfactory sense in her brain to bring it back. Such love! I have never been loved like that. And his voice! The timbre of it, soothing and vibrating in her mind. *'I could never forget the way in which he spoke,'* she thought.

"Why did it have to be a dream?" she exclaimed. Closing her eyes again, seeking to reclaim that moment of being taken into his arms. "Take me away with you," - the last murmuring recall of the dream fluttering away.

Dawn peeked around the corner of the curtains, pushing further aside the night vision of love. The sun rose brilliant, brighter, just a bleached reflection of her night's encounter. Taking a deep breath, Shula pushed the bed clothes away, unwilling to leave the beautiful dream behind, but life beckoned.

Quickly going through her morning routine, Shula showered, dressed ready for work, and then made her first morning coffee.

Looking out of the window at the beauty of the sky, she absently reached for her Bible and flicked it open randomly.

"Ha! Song of Solomon. I've never really read that," she said. "I've always wondered why it was in the Bible. It feels very explicit!" She giggled and started reading, occasionally sipping her coffee.

"Let him kiss me with the kisses of his mouth - for your love is more delightful than wine. Pleasing is the fragrance of your perfume..." she stopped reading; her head jerked back, and she yelped in surprise. "That's my dream! OMIGOSH, that's my dream," her voice was shaky, disbelieving. "Lord?" Shula looked around the room as though she would see Jesus standing there. A fluttery feeling in her tummy accompanied her amazement.

"What! How can that be?" She read the passage again, and the dream tendrils seemed to come forward, the images growing ever more real.

Closing her eyes, Shula sought again the seeming elusive night encounter, inhaling deeply the aroma of his presence which seemed to wrap around her, recapturing its essence.

Worlds and universes, unimaginable galaxies, suns and stars spun past Shula, as she floated out of time and space. An awareness that her body was still seated in the lounge chair washed fleetingly over her, but it felt inconsequential for her spirit was alive. Fresh, renewed, completely awake and conscious.

The sound of water falling into a pool rushed past her ears and the redolent odour of trees and water and hot rocks spiced the air.

"Shula." The same voice of her dream called her.

She opened her eyes. What a splendid garden! There, over there; that was the source of the sound of falling water. Shula looked carefully at it. The water seemed to be alive, having its own presence. Tinkling laughter as the water fell, fell, fell, baptising the pool it cascaded in to.

And sitting over there, smiling at her, was her Beloved from the dream.

Her Beloved stayed where He was on the other side of the garden. She looked again at Him.

Shula walked across the soft grass, and kneeling before him, inhaled his fragrance. "Am I dreaming again?" she asked Beloved. "Because if I am dreaming, I never want to waken."

He smiled down at her, his adoration for her shown plainly.

Yeshua reached out to touch His precious one, His own that He had purchased with His life. Shula took His hand and kissed it, her lips caressing the scars on the palm, brushing across the ring with me in it.

In that moment, she knew who He was, who she was, and closing her eyes, again inhaled the fragrance, the essence, that surrounded Him.

"Lord," was all Shula could say.

The trees in the garden whispered it back to her:

'Lord, He is Lord, He is Lord, He is Lord.'

"I'm always with you, Shula. There has never been a moment that I have left you. Peace now. We will meet again."

He touched her gently with the back of his hand, caressing her cheek.

Absent-mindedly, Shula reached for her coffee, startled by her action, and startled to find it still hot.

Had she fallen asleep again? Was it a dream?

Shaking her head, she turned back to her morning reading in the Song of Solomon. She read from verse 10, "Your cheeks are beautiful with earrings, and your neck with strings of jewels." There, right in the middle of the verse was a little pink heart shaped gem. "Where did that come from?" She asked out loud.

~~~ 🐑 ♡ 🐑 ~~~

We watched Shula's bemusement and Yeshua laughed with delight, clapping His hands in joy, for His beloved was starting to wake up.

While the king
was at His table,
my perfume
spread its fragrance.
My lover is to me
a sachet of myrrh resting
between
my breasts.
My lover is to me
a cluster of henna
blossoms from
the vineyard
of En Gedi.
Song of Solomon 1:12-15

6

How can mankind forget so quickly? Why couldn't Shula remember BEFORE, before when she lived with us? I marvel constantly at how tender Yeshua is with Shula, beckoning to her, calling her forward to Himself. *'Let the king take me into his chambers.'* Oh, My Lord so longs for Shula, and yet He must restrain Himself, allowing His Father's timetable to work out.

In the distance, I could hear the chorus from the dream being repeated as all of Heaven, angels, creatures and mankind caught the refrain, and I joined in singing with them:

We rejoice and delight in you
We will praise your love more than wine
How right it is to adore you

It brought back memories of my time on earth, when just the merest breath of worship to Almighty God turned my heart back again to Heaven. It was a time to stop, to notice the nuances woven in the wind.

Yeshua felt my thoughts as I sat securely on His finger. He is so attuned to all that is being thought and felt. My little heart that was once stone, burst into joyful praise and we both laughed as the joy in my heart and mind changed the resonance of love into a myriad of brilliant colours. I loved watching the colours emanating from my Lord. For all beings have their own frequency and resonance.

Yeshua stood. He was listening intently, and because there is no time, and no distance in Him, we were instantly in a different place.

Across the Sea of Glass that was made from a single precious stone, upon which the rain of the Almighty constantly fell, voices called out in ecstasy, praises rebounding from one side of the sea to the other, reaching up high into the Holy Hill. The Angels, together with Mankind, wove their melodies united in purest praise.

Myriads of tiny babies, whose destinies had been cut off, were carried in the arms of angels, and with whole families clustered together, multiple generations all worshiped the great Creator.

Holy Spirit, wove in and out of the worshippers, the rainbow essence embracing and settling on the assembly, touching all, while Moses' deep baritone rumbled along with the highest soprano of the choir. Glory mist dripped off those present.

The love from God for His creation emanated as a tidal wave towards His people, meeting the wave of love from the worshippers pouring back to Him. The wave curled up. Up like a wave on a beach, meeting at the top as though with interlaced fingers, and then flooding back over the great crowd. Living waters flowed from under the Throne, spilling out and engulfing, overflowing and immersing all who chose to step into the torrent of life-giving, refreshing, waters.

The stones on the Son's breastplate rang forth their resonance, reflecting their earthly counterparts, while Melchizedek radiated righteousness, his glory throbbing a brilliant white light.

Trembling notes drifted away as the fullness of silence settled.

Yeshua walked among His people eagerly looking into their hearts and seeing His bride forming; the radiant glow on many faces meeting His desire and fuelling His love for these Cherished Ones.

"Soon," He sang. "Soon it will be my marriage supper." Singing His heart's song toward His beloved, the longing for His beloved radiating out in His voice.

7

Dearest Shula,

You are the entire purpose of this earth, for it was created just for you. Search for Truth, Shula. You will find her, and when you find her, you will find me, for I am the only way, I am the only truth, I am the only substance of Life you will ever need.

Yeshua stopped writing and seemed to stare at nothing, but the reality is that I knew He was looking through time and distance which do not exist in our realm, and looking for His bride.

He picked His pen up again and continued writing His love letter.

Did you know that you are as strong as one of the mares harnessed to a golden chariot? No, you are even stronger, for you are a pillar of great strength. For in your training, you, my beloved, will find that you will truly become my helpmate. You inhabit the turrets and towers of a great castle.

I felt Yeshua's hand tremble, and I looked at Him. Tears were running down His face, and I knew how His heart ached for His Beloved to know Him. To know Him and to know who she truly is.

How beautiful you are, my darling. Oh, how beautiful! Your eyes are as soft as doves.

He wrote again using analogies she would understand, for the eyes of a dove were indeed very soft and pure; a dove such as had been used in the Temple as a blood sacrifice. Until Yeshua, that is. For now, the time of blood sacrifices was over. When He had completed His journey and cried out "IT IS FINISHED", all Heaven, hell and earth trembled with that knowledge. Yeshua continued writing,

My love bird with dove's eyes, for did you know, my Shula, that when a dove fixes its gaze on its mate, it is not distracted by any activities around it? How I long for your eyes to be fixed on me.

My heart swelled at the imagery Yeshua was using. How could Shula fail to be wooed by this? And the dove. Oh, the beautiful dove; the symbol of Holy Spirit, Ruach Ha'Kodesh.

Yeshua started writing again.

When I gave myself to ransom you from the wicked one, you were all I thought of. You, as a beautiful lily growing among thorns, you are all my Father and I have thought of, and now the rescue of my Darling is almost complete. Remember who you are, Shula. Remember me.

Always beloved, I am yours.
Yeshua.

A single tear fell off His cheek and plopped into the middle of the letter, falling on the word 'bride'. I watched as the word grew and enlarged and changed form, becoming great in its meaning, expanding until the Living Letters shimmered and sparkled, weaving in and out of Shula, the Betrothed – She who holds the turrets and towers of the high places; she who was being fitted to rule and reign with Yeshua.

Then Yeshua smiled. "Oh yes, Beryl. This is the true meaning. My people do not know who they are, but their understanding is being enlarged and changed."

He then kissed me and pressed His kiss onto the letter, sealing it with His covenant promise.

The closer I got to the heart of Yeshua, the clearer my lustre shone. And then I looked at Shula and saw that her radiance was clouded, but right in the centre was a tiny space that shone with the light of Heaven. It was into that space that Yeshua was pouring His love; cleaning, clearing and expanding.

Now there was only the fulfilment of completion to bringing Shula home.

8

On earth, the night grew bold and Shula yawned sleepily. It had been a long day and she was weary; ready for bed and sleep. Slowly, the peace and blessing of rest fell on her, and her body and mind relaxed into sleep.

My Lord looked at Shula. In Him there is no time, no distance. Though she could not yet see Him, He stood in front of her. Reaching out, He caressed her cheek. Yeshua pushed back the tendrils of dreaming, just as he pushed back the tendrils of Shula's hair and called her to Himself.

Shula stirred in her sleep, responding to her lover's voice, but the depths of sleep claimed her, pulling her deeply into its rest.

"Arise my darling, my beautiful one, and come with me. The time of singing has come. Come with me." Yeshua called her again.

The Lord called her, His voice becoming softer, but more insistent, and then He started to sing to her.

"Come into my garden
And see all my creation
Come into my presence
And see what I have done
See all of the fields
Ready for the planting
Tender loving shoots grow
Under my watchful care
Breathe deep inside my love
Breathe deep inside my Spirit.
Look at all the trees
The pruning and the planting
Will yield a crop of love
Soaking in my presence
Rest under my love
The shade under my branches
Sheltered from the storm.

Nourished in my love
Come dream with me my love
Come dance inside my garden
Listen to the breeze
Blowing through the garden
The cry of my heart's song
Calling out to you
The weeds of webs have disappeared
I've cleared a path for you
Unwoven threads, rekindled life
Awaken to new life
Awaken, oh my love
Awaken in my Spirit."

(* Lyrics by Juanita Anderson)

My radiance glowed under Yeshua's call to Shula, for does not all creation respond to that pure love? His perfume became stronger, and of its own volition, rose from His being, formed into an aromatic cloud and then spread itself over Shula.

"Good," He said. "Now you carry my aroma and all who meet you know whose you are. Your love calls to me and causes me to respond." He bent down and kissed her gently on her cheek. "Remember Shula. Remember me."

We sat for a while longer, watching this most precious of all creation sleep.

"Guard her well," the Lord of All instructed Shula's angels.

They bowed as we left Shula's room and ascended into the garden of the Lord.

Shula stirred in her sleep, her eyelids flittering, responding to her inner thoughts. "Jesus," she called. "Wait for me."

In deep sleep her heart searched for Him whom she was falling in love with.

"All is well, my beloved. I will write to you again," He told her.

9

We stood in the place where there is no time, where the past is the present and also the future, for God exists outside of time.

Yeshua watched in delight as Adam and his family moved freely between the place known as Eden and our home here in Heaven.

The entire family were clothed in light, made in the same form and frequency as Father God; the radiance of the rainbow around the throne reflecting Holy Spirit, being the covering glory of all mankind. The prisms of colour moved and rippled as they moved.

Yeshua clapped His hands joyfully.

Adam and Father talked together. Father took Adam to a tree, a beautiful tree, and cautioned him never to touch this fruit. Adam understood. It wasn't about the fruit; it wasn't even about obedience to his Father. It was about the entire future of all creation resting on this pivotal point.

Sadly, Adam and his family did disobey. For the beautiful creature who twisted and distorted truth told them only half the story. And the intrinsic lies of the evil one entered Adam's family, thus beginning the degeneration of man's D.N.A.

Down through the millennia we watched as the glory covering became partially obscured. Sickness, famine, disease and death entered. The glory now looked as though the finest piece of white linen had been dragged through mud, trodden carelessly underfoot, so that just the merest hint of glow surrounded each person.

I had been so engrossed in watching, that I was startled to see that many angels had gathered with us to watch. They were silent, for even though they had seen this many times before, the gravity of sin and war entering our home had also pierced their hearts. That our own could betray us was beyond our comprehension.

A quick flash and splash of red, the red of the frequency of the rainbow, caused the angels to jump back. Yeshua laughed, enjoying the moment when His sacrifice startled Creation and caused the rebirth back to Eden.

A groaning came from the Earth as the red blood dripped onto her outer mantle. The blood spread over mankind, and some were seen walking again, clothed in Holy Spirit glory, their garments of white restored.

But few of them understood who they were. They were like the dirty Spirit-linen covering they had all worn. It had gradually lost its shape and memory of where they had originally come from.

Do not the Holy writings say that as Yeshua is now, glorified and seated with His Father, so are those who carry His name?

Sadly, Shula no longer remembered. But the Lord was awakening her to His love.

"Remember," He constantly said to her.

"Remember whose you are."

My dove in the clefts
of the rock,
in the hiding places
on the mountainside,
show me your face.
Let me hear your voice
for your voice is sweet
and your face is lovely.
Catch for us the foxes,
the little foxes
that ruin the vineyards;
our vineyards
that are in bloom.
Song of Solomon 2:14-15

10

Dearest Shula,

Did you see the rainbow I sent you? Every one of the colours tells of my love for you, a message within a message. Did you know that all the colours have their own frequency? And every frequency tells a story of my passion for you.

Did you also know that there is a rainbow around the throne of my Father, and that beautiful Holy Spirit is clad in the colours of the rainbow? So therefore, why should I not speak to you in a rainbow?

See, look at the analogy I have given you. Where there is rain, there will be a rainbow. In the same way, Shula, where there is a season of rain in your life, look for my rainbow. I am always there. I will always show you signposts so you can find your way.

Look again in delight when you see my message to you in the clouds. Did you know that not only do the colours have meaning, but also their frequency, as well? The rainbow we put on the earth, is the same reflection of the rainbow around my Father's throne. It is the same rainbow that Holy Spirit is clothed in, and if you could only see yourself, you also are clothed in the rainbow. I, your love, your Lord, your Yeshua, I Am the rainbow, for I am light. I embody the entire spectrum of light. All light from me comes as though through a prism and shines out as all the colours of the rainbow: luminous energy, radiant light.

Let me tell you about the colours. Let me weave the story of my love for you so often seen in the rainbow, but not understood.

All the colours tell a story. The red of course is my blood that covers you, and therefore has the longest wavelength. My blood speaks to all eternity, echoes through all there is, as a testimony of my redemption of you and all of creation. It is all about my love which transcends time and eternity.

The red blends into orange, a combination of red and yellow. It has been said that the Spirit of Wisdom is clothed in orange. Such a warm and vibrant colour. What do you see, Shula? When you call on Wisdom, how do you see her gowned? Is not fire orange? Wisdom is ablaze with all that my Father imbues on those who ask for her. She is part of my Father, part of His glory.

The glory of my Father is likened as gold and this is reflected in the rainbow as the beautiful, glorious yellow colour. That colour that is indescribable, for how does one describe glory? Did you know, my Shula, that the sun is not yellow at all, but all the colours of the rainbow?

"Me, me, me, Yeshua," I interrupted Him. "Remember my colour, for I am a mix of orange and yellow as well. Beryl means wise and pure."

Yeshua chuckled. "Everything has meaning, doesn't it, Beryl?" He turned back to his letter to Shula.

One of the most beautiful colours, Shula, is green. Have you ever wondered at the many variations of green in nature? The purity of life reflected in a new shoot, a new blade of grass. It starts out as a lighter shade and deepens as it matures. Such is righteousness, peace, and new growth in me. The merging of yellow and blue brings about the lovely shade of green.

Yeshua stopped writing and smiled. I knew He was thinking about creation, for everything that the Lord created is a reflection of Heaven. How I had missed Heaven when I was on earth, for the colours on earth have been diluted by sin. But here, in Heaven, colours are vivid, they are alive, reflecting all the glory of the Father. "'Think, Shula, think," I silently begged her. "Look around you and wonder. See who you are, who you were created to be."

"I agree, Beryl," Yeshua said. "I long for my Beloved to remember who she is, that she, in her beauty, reflects the rainbow. In fact, she emits rainbow light. Oh, I long for my Bride." Yeshua knew my every thought and the longings of my heart. I could only guess at how much He yearned for the time of fulfilment, when Shula would become the Bride.

He turned back to His letter.

Blue. Heavenly, beautiful blue, Shula. My Father's throne is made from blue sapphire. A royal, Holy colour.

It is a colour that has been used in the Temple. A colour of my divinity. Look Shula, look at the rainbow again and understand my heart. And blue merges into Indigo. Indigo is like a bridge between the finite and the infinite, where Violet reflects the purple of splendour, of majesty and expresses fullness, for Indigo is the furthest from the red of my blood, and takes us to the grandeur of Almighty God.

All these colours are our promise to you, a promise that has never been broken and never shall be broken. From the time of Noah, my Father put His very presence in the rainbow, so when you would look and see the bow of colour in the sky, you would know you were seeing the rainbow around my Father.

Shula, think on this. Think of Holy Spirit when the tongues of fire anointed the heads of my people, flames of fire, the colours of orange, and yellow, and blue, and green and indigo and violet. All the colours of the flame of fire that was in the rainbow in that one event.

The rainbow is the spirit of glory, of Holy Spirit. The Spirit of God is dressed in the rainbow, and thus, when you are baptised in Holy Spirit, you also wear the rainbow. The rainbows around my Father's throne sing and dance. Every colour contains its own melody. Listen. Can you hear it?

Father said 'I have set my rainbow into the earth as my promise.' And this is my promise to you, my Beloved: My Beloved is mine, and I am hers. No one can snatch my Beloved out of my hand.

Pausing to think for a moment, He continued to write, and what He wrote surprised me, but it made absolutely perfect sense.

You will have seen a growing group of people all calling themselves the 'people of the rainbow.' I know it has grieved your heart. You feel they have stolen something pure and beautiful and eliminated one of the colours but, my Beloved, do not grieve; laugh as my Father and I do, for every time they declare they are rainbow people, they are declaring MY TRUTH! My truth never changes. It continues to resound throughout earth and eternity. As they declare the rainbow, they are declaring me and I have called them into my Kingdom.

Yeshua stopped writing and together we read over what He had explained to Shula. Satisfied that His love was shown in every colour, He kissed me and pressed His kiss onto the letter containing His heart's love.

~~~ ❦ ♡ ❧ ~~~

The rain finally drizzled its way to the finish and the clouds drifted off to drop their rain on someone else.

Shula went out to the sodden garden, inhaling the rain-cleansed air. Tilting her head back, she closed her eyes, breathing deeply and enjoying the ozone aroma after the rain.

"That's so good," she remarked to the trees, the grass, the flowers. "I love that clean smell after the rain." Holding her arms out she twirled around, enjoying the feeling of her skirt swishing around and falling again on her legs. "Look at the sky. I'm glad to see you again, blue sky." She laughed as she spoke to the sky, knowing full well that it couldn't hear her. Patches of blue were appearing as the clouds thinned and leaves on the trees dripped their rain diamonds onto the ground. Shula watched droplets fall, admiring their mirroring the iridescent sheen of a pearl. The sun caught a large drop of water wavering on the edge of a leaf. A prism of light shot the drop through with rainbow colours.

"Oh, how utterly beautiful," Shula's eyes widened at the unexpected artistry of God. She stood quite still, wanting to capture the moment, to stay in that place of awe. "Lord, that is wonderful," she acknowledged the Creator. "How I wish I could stay in the wonder of this moment of time forever. A tiny rainbow, just for me."

Yeshua stood by her, smiling, all His courting and wooing of Shula present in that moment.

11

"My Lord." Michael and Gabriel bowed low before the King.

Jesus smiled at Michael, his trusted Chief of Heaven's armies, and Gabriel, who stands before the throne of God, the messenger carrier, the change bringer.

"It is time. It is time to free my bride from the shackles of centuries of misconstrued understanding and show her who she is." The King did an excited little jig around the table. "For too long now, the nameless one has blinded my people as to who they are, and who I am. Now it is time for truth, and you," He nodded at Michael and Gabriel, "will of course, be my First Assistants in this."

Turning to the viewing screen, the King of all Kings commanded, "Adam."

Both Angels and the Lord stood watching in delight, revisiting that time, as the first man, Adam, was formed in absolute perfection, a replica in every way of the image of God Himself. Not just in form, but as an imager of the Creator, to be a mirror and show the world the Father.

"As I am now, so are they," Yeshua murmured. "And yet, they do not understand this, nor do they know who they are."

The man stood while Ruach Ha'Kodesh, Holy Spirit, wreathed the rainbow from the throne around him, the prisms of light blending perfectly colour into colour, their different wavelengths commensurate with his status as being made just a little lower than God. Made to have dominion over the earth and all creation, to rule and reign in harmony and authority, crowned by the Lord God Himself, with glory and honour.

As Adam moved freely between earth and heaven's realms, his garment, made of purest light shimmered with great lustre, the violet sheen echoing Ruach Ha'Kodesh through the spectrum of colour, the rainbow radiance moving and rippling like Holy Spirit.

In time, the Father presented the woman to Adam, and he named her Eve, she from whom breath and life for all would come, the quickening of the Bride.

For time, and more time, the first two of God's creation, those whom he called elohim after Himself, ran through the glorious garden, crossing through between dimensions with no thought of the difference, for truly, there was none.

In sorrow, the Lord and His arch-angels watched the betrayal. They watched the replay of the first animal sacrifice God had made, to cover the two humans. For now, their light covering was undone. God slew an animal. Blood was shed, the red of the rainbow spilling onto the ground. In agony of heart, the Father forced them out of the garden and into a harsh realm, and in anguish, shut the portals between the realms.

Down through millennia, the journey of mankind was played out, their glory covering now torn and tattered, filthy.

The blood of the Messiah flowed across creation and out into universes, galaxies and into the realms of forever. Earth groaned, trembling as the red blood soaked into her. Tombs were broken open and those long dead were seen walking through the streets of Jerusalem.

Dots of glory started spreading across the entire earth.

Jesus smiled. "These are my betrothed." Some of those light bearers' garments shone brighter than the others. "These ones have remembered who they are," He said.

Through many ages, lights flickered and went out. The rainbow glory grew distorted as man sought to subjugate mankind; lies, gnarly twisted truths becoming half-truths and finally, no truth. Very few brilliant lights remained and those who carried the light were persecuted, the brilliant linen lights again becoming sullied with man's teaching replacing freedom.

Yeshua spoke. "There will always be a remnant," He said, indicating the few bright lights scattered across the world.

We watched as faith revivals came and went, always being hi-jacked by man, twisted for his own control and advantage, and finally disappearing as though a mist had diluted them away.

There was silence in the War Room as the viewing screen ceased its action.

"My beautiful ones!" Jesus whispered. "Now it is time for the Betrothed to remember who they are. Michael, get your Angels ready, and Gabriel, I have many messages for you to deliver."

Dark am I, yet lovely,
O daughters of Jerusalem,
dark like the
tents of Kedar;
like the tent curtains
of Solomon.
Do not stare at me
because I am dark
because I am darkened
by the sun.
My mother's sons
were angry with me
and made me take care
of the vineyards;
my own vineyard
I have neglected.
Song of Solomon 1:5-6

12

Shula set the alarm for an hour earlier than normal, determined to do what she had heard others say was right: Get up early, read her Bible, and pray. As the alarm shrilled her awake, she groggily reached out and turned the horrible noise off. "Just another five minutes," she muttered, and without noticing, she drifted back to sleep, only to jerk awake half an hour after her normal wake up time.

"Oh no. I'm going to be late for work!" Scrambling out of bed, taking the fastest shower ever, and without time for breakfast, Shula drove off to work. Stuck in the rush hour traffic, she wailed to the Lord, "I'm sorry, I truly was going to get up, but bed was so nice.

I promise I'll get up early tomorrow. Please forgive me. I will try harder."

Yeshua watched as His beloved poured her heart out to Him. "My bride, I only want you. I want to talk with you, to share your life," He told her. But Shula did not hear. She had not trained herself to listen.

The Angel in the passenger seat winced at Shula's lack of understanding of what it meant to seek after Yeshua. Another of Shula's Angels who was hanging out the window enjoying the ride, shrugged. "Religion," he said. "It binds these humans and destroys the life out of them. Our Lord knows exactly what He is doing."

When the alarm woke Shula the next morning, she determinedly turned it off and got straight out of bed. Making her morning coffee, she sat in her chair and reached for her Bible. "One chapter," she yawned, I must read a chapter." Doggedly, she started right at the beginning, Genesis chapter one, a book she could almost recite without having to read the text. The black letters on the white page seemed so dull, but the Pastor had said they were light and life, and to know God we have to know His Word. So, she read, *'In the beginning, God created the heavens and the earth.'* Drowsily Shula sipped at her coffee and continued reading the account of creation. *'God saw all that he had made, and it was very good. And there was evening, and there was morning – the sixth day.'*

She shut her Bible and put it on the coffee table. Then closing her eyes, Shula tried to pray, just as she had heard others pray. Big words, long prayers, praying for everyone, and she repented for every sin she could think of, everything she may have even thought which may have been wrong; said sorry for cutting that person off at the intersection yesterday. It felt forced and fake. How can people possibly find God this way? Her mind kept wandering and she kept coming back, "Lord, forgive me, I should be spending this time only for you." Again and again, her mind veered off looking at the sunrise, the trees, smiling at the birds, and wondering what she should have for dinner that night. And every time, she would beg forgiveness, for if she couldn't keep her mind focused on God, then she was failing. A thought popped into her mind, that maybe she should pray for herself, but instantly dismissed that as being self-centred and selfish. There were many other people far more in need of prayer that her, she reasoned.

Shula didn't see Jesus sitting in the tree. She didn't see His glory in the sunrise. She couldn't see the Angels flying with the birds. And she didn't see the light leaping off the pages of her Bible. She saw only her failure. But she did feel that she had accomplished something. *I did it. I got out of bed on time. I read my Bible, and I prayed.*

But, unfulfilled, frustrated at her lack of progress, Shula gave up on the seeking God idea for that day. It had felt utterly fruitless and unfulfilling. She didn't get any great revelations, nor had she noticed any light or life jumping off her Bible. "Thank the Lord, it's finally Friday," she muttered, getting ready for work.

The next morning, with no alarm to wake her, she revelled in the delicious feeling of Saturday. Oh! The luxury of knowing she didn't have to get up and go to work today. Bed felt so good. She looked at her watch. 7:30. Still early.

Quietly, she got out of bed, dragging her dressing-gown on and shoving her feet into her slippers, she softly made her way out to the lounge room, shutting the door behind her so as to block any noise. *Coffee first,* she thought, *and then to do my quiet time with God.*

"Could this be any more boring?" Shula said aloud, as she flipped through some pages of the Bible. Nothing stood out. Nothing seemed right.

How can people find this exciting, she thought. *I gave my heart to Jesus so long ago, and I've never found this interesting. Oh! I give up. I just can't do what I'm supposed to do.*

Worthlessness sat on her shoulder. Aloud she said, "I'm useless. I just can't do this. I give up."

Frustrated, she let her Bible slip off her lap onto the floor, where it fell, on its face, twisted and upside down with the pages turned under its weight. Shula slumped in her chair, utterly spent. Slow tears formed and fell. A moan of defeat and failure groaned from deep inside her.

"Pleasing is the fragrance of your perfume," she tried to pray. "Oh, what's the use!" she yelled. "I'm so tired. I've been fighting for so long and there's no let up. What is the point?"

"Lord, I can't even read your Word. What is wrong with me?" Sobbing, Shula's heart cried out to God. "Help me, please help me. I'm sorry. I'm no good at this. I can't do what I'm supposed to do. I want to give up. How am I supposed to serve you if I find the Bible boring and praying is just so dull and lifeless?"

Guilt piled on top of her. She *should* be able to at least read her Bible. What sort of Christian was she?

The feeling of inadequacy filled her with shame and self-loathing. Her brow was creased, eyes reflecting the inward pain. Everything that she had ever learned in church, from those who must obviously have a lot more knowledge than she had. They must have something special. She didn't have it. It all came down to this moment in time. And she could not comply with the church-rules. She just couldn't do it. She was a failure.

In the other realm, the Lord looked at Shula and signalled to the angels with Him. "Peace, go to her now. I would not have my beloved in such distress." The Spirit of Peace bowed.

Courage bowed to the King. "My Lord, shall I also go to her?"

"Yes, Courage. Impart my strength to her so she will want to push in to find me." Tears slid down the King's face. His heart was in agony as He watched His precious one wrestling with half-truths that had been deliberately created to keep her in bondage. How angry He was at the evil one.

Peace and Courage left Yeshua and slipped unseen through the veil to stand by Shula.

They bowed their heads in honour of the Lord's Beloved. Peace reached out and touched her heart; that which she carried from the Lord being freely given to Shula. Courage put both his hands on her head and whispered, "The Master imparts of His courage to you."

~~~ ❧ ♡ ☙ ~~~

Sighing in resignation, Shula bent over and picked her Bible up, turning it over to where it had fallen.

Courage quickly rearranged the fluttering pages.

Smoothing the bent pages out, the Beloved read: *'I slept but my heart was awake.'* Her eyes flicked to the top of the page: "Song of Solomon." Intrigued, she continued to read, and when she came to verse seven: *'The watchmen found me as they made their rounds in the city. They beat me and bruised me; they took away my cloak.'*

"Wow," Shula spoke aloud to herself. "Those who were supposed to protect her, actually violated her."

Yeshua nodded. "YES!" He exclaimed. "Look again. Read it again and understand."

Using her finger to follow the letters, Shula read the passage again, not seeing that the letters were alive, living letters.

Yeshua despatched the Spirit of Understanding to her. Understanding stood beside Shula and opened her heart to receive Truth.

"'I slept but my heart was awake, Listen, my Lover is knocking,' Oh! That's how I felt the other night. I was asleep and Jesus, I could feel you calling, but I just couldn't wake up. Wow!" Her lips moved as she whispered the words of Song of Solomon 5:2-7 again. "'My hands dripped with myrrh.' What does that mean, Lord?" she asked.

Yeshua walked through the curtain between the realms to be with Shula.

Shula continued to read, trying to understand the symbolism within the age-old words. Slowly, she became aware of a faint resinous, almost pine scented aroma around her.

Smiling, Yeshua said, "That is myrrh, Beloved."

And she read again: "'I looked for him.' That's like you, Jesus. I keep looking for you. I'm doing what I thought I was supposed to do to find you and I couldn't find you in that way. But now, randomly, I feel your presence so close to me." Shula sat for a moment in wonder, eyes not seeing what was around her, looking inwardly at the revelation of God.

Jesus chuckled. "Yes, very close, my Shula. Right by you with my perfume dripping off you. Now, read more and understand."

The Spirit of Understanding nodded at Yeshua and held her hands over Shula's heart. Breathing on her, Understanding whispered, "There is freedom in Truth, Shula. Receive Understanding."

"Why would the watchmen, who were supposed to protect the people, beat her up? Why would they do that?" Shula wondered.

As she read that stanza again, she saw something else. *'...they beat me, they bruised me, they took away my cloak.'* "OH!" That's prophesy! Jesus, that's what they did to you! And it was the religious leaders that instigated it. But why?"

Understanding smiled. "Keep thinking about this, Shula. You are almost there."

Reading again, slowly, her finger following every word, Shula struggled to see behind what she had always been taught. Why had she never seen the parallels between Jesus' treatment and what was essentially a love story? Why did those who were supposed to protect the Shulamite woman, instead beat her up?

"Why have I never seen this before, Lord?"

Truth blew on Shula. "Receive TRUTH, Shula," she said. "Look higher, Shula."

"Watchmen," she murmured to herself. "What is the modern-day equivalent of a watchman? Police? No, not when we are talking about things of God. Think Shula. Think!" she gave herself instructions. "Ok, what would be the corresponding authority in

Jesus' time?" She drummed her feet on the carpet, thinking hard, trying to draw the parallels.

Yeshua and I watched as Shula slowly worked her way through the quagmire of conditioning beliefs, sorting out the poetry of the Song and tentatively finding her way towards Yeshua's truth. I loaned all my faith to hers, adding my God-given glory to Yeshua, so that my facets shone brilliantly.

Shula thought of all the leaders she knew and had known. All the ministers, the pastors and all those who had been held in authority over her. With some, she smiled at their wonderful caring, and others caused anxiety to rise up. Scenes flashed into her mind, scenes where she felt like a failure, not good enough, unable to comply with demands. Times where she couldn't quite understand what she was expected to be or to do. She felt she had failed those people, failed to follow the rules they had made sound so simple; do this and you will get that. If you don't do this, then you run the risk of eternal damnation. Or you will be outside the perfect will of God, and that would be bad. You must do this, or that, to be acceptable.

Heart pounding, Shula moaned slightly, going into the heightened state known as anxiety. "Forgive me Lord, I have failed you, Lord. I'm sorry, I haven't done what you want me to do."

Yeshua was angry. Angry at what the enemy had done to His beautiful bride. Angry at how man had twisted and distorted His words. Angry at those who had put demands on His children, and crushed their soft hearts. Angry at those who sought to subjugate His little ones.

But His heart was gentle and soft before Shula. He knelt and put His arms around her.

"Beloved, tell me who the watchmen are?" He whispered into her heart, drawing her back to His side.

Her heart caught His words. Taking a deep breath to steady herself, she read the verse yet again. Understanding blew on her again, Truth pushed aside the cobwebs of lies and a tiny blink of light formed in Shula's heart.

"That is not me, Shula. I have never enforced rules and religion on you. It is not Truth. It is not Righteousness. You will never become righteous through following a list of rules and man's ideas. Follow me. I alone bring life, light, and freedom. Any doctrine or belief that brings fear and condemnation is not from me."

The blink of light grew to become a small glow.

Oh, how I danced. My Lord was setting Shula free. How my heart rejoiced to see mankind untangled from webs of deceit and enslavement. My facets gleamed brightly, shooting out their orange and yellow frequencies, calling on the Rainbow to dance with me.

Yeshua spoke again, "Religious leaders are caught up in rules and 'religion'. They are lacking relationship. You will only find me through intimate relationship with me. I long for you Shula."

Stifling her sobs, Shula's heart started to open, allowing her the freedom to, at last, find her Lover, the lover in her dreams, the reality of Yeshua.

"Lord," she cried. "Thank you. You always know what I need."

Courage smiled and Peace stroked her hair, watching as the weight of tiredness lifted and the Master's Peace, Joy and Courage took root in her heart and spread through her. They looked through the veil and saw the great crowd of witnesses smiling back.

Shula, the beloved, had started to walk to the heart of the Father. She was encouraged again, and her strength was returning. Heaven rejoiced.

She sighed with delicious relief as the peace settled over her, wrapping her mind and heart in the softest embrace. Her shoulders dropped as her body relaxed in response to the peace. "Lord, how I love you," she cried and got up, pirouetting around the lounge room, arms outstretched as though reaching for another. "Let him kiss me with the kisses of his mouth. Your love is intoxicating." Shula giggled. "Jesus, why was the Song of Solomon included in the Bible? It's a bit raunchy!"

And going about her work, she danced and sang, using the vacuum cleaner as her pseudo microphone, her garment of light shimmering as she moved.

Unseen, unfelt by Shula, Jesus slipped from that realm to the earth realm and kissed Shula gently on the forehead. He smiled at her abandoned dancing for Him, murmuring back to her whispers of love "Oh how beautiful you are, my darling bride. But how angry I am at the nameless one for entrapping my beloved in a tangle of deceit." He moved right in front of Shula who had stopped her dancing and stood with her arms by her side, head lifted as though looking through the veil to heaven, eyes closed.

"I am going to free you, my beloved, from all these rules you have been taught to follow, and teach you that I only want your love, your company. This man-made system has slapped, bruised and beaten my people instead of releasing them into my freedom and the realisation of who they are. Now, let's get these little foxes who are ruining your vineyard."

I opened for my lover,
but my lover had left;
he was gone
My heart sank
at his departure
I looked for him
but did not find him.
I called him
but he did not answer.
The watchmen found me
as they made their rounds
in the city
They beat me,
they bruised me;
they took away my cloak,
those watchmen of the walls
Song of Solomon 5:6 - 7

13

A single, loud, long note resounded from the trumpet, echoing again and again, rebounding off ancient stars, carrying from universe to galaxy, on into places mankind has not yet discovered exist. The note continued on and on, resonating deep within us all until it pounded through every cell and molecule of all beings. The purest note of אמת *TRUTH* burst forth and smashed the screaming of lies. We listened as the sound of false beliefs shattered, bringing freedom to Shula.

As though a tangible object, the lies exploded outwards as thousands of pieces of light, gilded with the rainbow shot forth, hitting every target.

I, Beryl, watched in awe as the deception encasing Shula's mind cracked and then fragmented like shards of delicate glass. Tiny bursts of light pierced each lie in her mind's belief system, falling off her, and collapsing like balloons that had been starved of air. Now harmless. As they hit the ground, poof, each lie disappeared in a smoggy foul cloud as so much insubstantial mist; back to where they had come from.

The shrieking of exposure from the demons was drowned out by the shout of Heaven's victory. The witnesses, the angels, and all the living creatures gave voice, their approval exploding out over heads, traveling through space and time, seeking out any crevice, any hiding place, though it was as a mere whisper compared to Yeshua's roar, proclaiming freedom.

Ten thousand times ten thousand voices intertwined together as one voice, giving a great cry of victory at the overthrowing of the evil one's kingdom.

He watched in satisfaction at the revealing to Shula of who He was.

Yeshua stood in eternity, and stretching forth His right hand, rearranged Shula's Timeline to reflect the changes. "You were taught incorrectly, my Beloved. You were not shown who you truly are, nor who I am.

For you, my Beloved, were created just a little lower than Us. Created to rule and co-create with Me.

Shula's Timeline danced with light, reflecting the Father, and she started to see who she was.

As Truth continued her journey, crossing from time into eternity, explosions could be heard as she hit each creature of evil, despatching their agenda, and revealing to the Beloved the fullness of Truth.

Yeshua's presence supernaturally altered the atmosphere around Shula. Sights and sounds totally changed. Every sound echoed a thousand times, reverberating and thrumming from the place where time exists, continuing on through to everlasting timelessness.

His roar echoed, vibrating out, causing waves of resonance to join in, riding the light which beamed out into the future. The perfume of the Lord cloaked all beings and everything, from the beginning of time, adorning the energy waves into the future.

"The perfume of heaven," I breathed in deeply, enjoying the beloved fragrance. "Even his name emits fragrance." I saw a glimpse of myself in Yeshua's breastplate and smiled to see the perfume dripping off me. Oh, I just love living so close to my Lord. What honour. What glory. The fulfilment of many, many days of pain. No more crying. No more tears. Joy, joy, joy.

I looked around. Michael stood, shifting foot to foot, as always impatient to get moving.

Angel after Angel moved into position behind their commanders. Finally, there was silence.

Michael bowed before Yeshua. "My Lord," he said. "I and the Angel Armies are ready."

The King of all Kings nodded, acknowledging Michael and the armies.

"Ride behind me," He said. "Follow my Standard. This is a new day."

The singers gathered in front of the army, their praise to Almighty God creating a highway on which the armies could march. As each note came from the mouth of a singer, it formed a physical presence and bowed before the King. The priests then came, all led by Melchizedek whose holy righteousness swirled about him, his staff of office and crown glistening, and giving off peels of thunder and great flashes of lightning. These manifestations joined in with the notes from the singers and broadened the path for the Armies of the Lord.

Yeshua's garment changed according to what the singers were decreeing in their songs, the stars in the skies lending their brilliance and the sun and moon bowed before Him. His robes of majesty glistened, woven from joy and glory, joining in with the throng gathered, all singing praises and pouring out their love to Yeshua.

"Arise!" He shouted. "Shake off the dust cloaking your mind, my people. For I will make your battlements of rubies and your gates of precious stones."

The singers, the priests, the angel armies shouted and cheered. All the great crowd of witnesses joined in, until everything in every realm shook.

The enemy who had held Shula in such bondage for so very long, scrambled to get away from the joy, the love, the abandonment of true freedom.

Yeshua shouted in laughter, then, holding His sceptre high, cried loudly, "Charge! Free my people!"

And the singers, the priests, the army, and all the people, the animals, Heaven's inhabitants ran at the enemy.

"Hashem shines," the roar from the realms of Heaven shook the court of the evil one.

"Free my people," Yeshua cried. "Let my people go."

It was a rout. The enemy lines could not hold against the fervour of Heaven. That which had already been written about the Lord's precious ones was once again in that great place of victory.

The enemy was forced to relinquish its hold over Shula. The chains of religion fell off and broke into tiny bits as they hit the ground.

"Now," said Yeshua, "Now comes the time of pruning."

~~~ ❧ ♡ ☙ ~~~

Something had changed in Shula's life. She couldn't quite put her finger on it, but ever since she'd read that passage in the Song of Solomon about the watchmen beating Shula instead of protecting her, she had started to see far more than ever before. It was as though she could see differently.

"New eyes," she said to herself. "I feel different. I actually want to read my Bible," she explained to a friend. "But I'm not doing what I always thought I had to do in order to know God. Somehow, I just know Him. And I *know* He loves me." She smiled, closing her eyes to enjoy the love she felt pulsating around her.

Looking inside herself, Shula thought, *'Oh, I long for you, Lord. I am yours, Lord, and you are mine. I hear you calling me now and my heart runs to you.'*

My lover is radiant and ruddy,
outstanding among ten
thousand,
His head is purest gold;
his hair is wavy
and black as a raven.
His eyes are like doves
by the water streams,
washed in milk,
mounted like jewels.
His cheeks are like beds of spice
yielding perfume.
His lips are like lilies
dripping with myrrh
His arms are rings of gold
set with Beryl.
His body is like polished ivory
decorated with sapphires.
Song of Solomon 5:10 - 14

14

"I can't explain it. It feels as though my mind has expanded." Shula struggled for the words to explain. "It's as though *I've* expanded. That I am suddenly far more aware of Jesus, as though He's right there beside me. As though I'm falling in love." She looked at Georgia fully expecting her to embrace this, for wasn't Georgia part of the church's leadership? But she didn't appear to have the faintest idea what Shula was talking about.

Georgia sipped her coffee, giving herself time to think. "What do you mean expanded?"

"Well, I had an experience with Jesus," Shula began, and then just stopped speaking, her mind going back to that moment. "Sorry. I haven't shared this with anyone else. I don't know who to talk to about it." Shula picked her coffee up, both elbows on the table and stared across the rim of the cup, her mind receding through time to her encounter with Yeshua.

Snapping her fingers, Georgia brought Shula's attention back. "Hello, earth to Shula, come in please."

Chewing her bottom lip, Shula started again. "I was reading through the Song of Solomon, and it just seemed to me that Jesus Himself popped in and gave me a personal Bible study. I've never seen it before, Georgia. I really can't explain it, but here, let me read you the passage and what He said to me."

Using her cell phone to find the passage in Song of Solomon 5:7, Shula read it to Georgia, describing her train of thought, how one thread led to another and the final understanding bringing freedom, and how Jesus Himself had taught her.

Georgia listened carefully, trying to slot what Shula was saying into her comprehension of what God was supposed to be, and what she had always known.

"Do you mean that you are saying that Jesus told you that the watchmen are like some church leaders?"

"Yes, that's exactly what it's like. That some are like the ones He called pharisees and hypocrites. That they are wounding their people instead of shepherding them.

Georgia stared at her. This was a most uncomfortable conversation. "Shula, thank you for sharing that with me." She put her hand on Shula's arm. "We have to be very careful about what voices we allow into our heads. Sometimes satan can manifest as an angel of light, and take us off track. My advice is to lay it out before God and just leave it. If it's God, then the pastor will be preaching the same thing."

Shula flinched. A jolt of anxiety spread through from her heart, blushing up her throat to her cheeks. Confusion entered very quietly, slowly stretching its claws throughout Shula's mind and firmly holding hands with anxiety.

"No, it's not like that, Georgia. It was Jesus. I know it was." Shula protested. Her back stiffened, her hands unconsciously holding each other as though to form a barricade against Georgia's words.

Doubt joined anxiety and confusion.

"It's only because I care, Shula. You know that the Bible says we need to correct one another in love. Thank you for sharing this with me. I will pray for you that you will be more careful in future." Georgia picked her bag up. "I'd better get home. Things to do." Standing up, she kissed Shula on the cheek, and walked away.

This was a blindside hit. Shula poked her tongue against the side of her cheek, trying to control herself, to not cry in public. Sitting in the cafe, she felt exposed, sure that everyone had seen the interaction, heard her humiliation and that they were all watching her.

'Lord, was I wrong? Was I wrong, Jesus? Tell me, please tell me. If I'm wrong, I really need to know. I was so sure it was you, Lord. But Georgia thinks I'm listening to the evil one. Not you. Lord, if I have this wrong, I'm so sorry. Please forgive me.'

Shula's thoughts were chaotic, filled with fear; tumbling recollections of her encounter now becoming jumbled.

"You got that one wrong," a voice sneered at her.

"Yesssss," hissed another voice. "You can't trust everything, you know. Better listen to Georgia."

Shula's angel clenched her fists, longing to put the nasty spirits to flight, but she had her orders, and understood why Shula had to go through this.

How angry my Lord was at this; another of the enemy's ploys designed to keep His beloved from her true inheritance. I am sure that my claw setting on the ring bristled also with indignation and anger. I flashed my warning, showing my red hues of anger at Lucifer. He couldn't destroy God's beautiful Heaven, so he was doing everything he could to destroy Shula.

Yeshua stroked me, the ring on His finger. "Yes Beryl. I know. I understand. But I have a plan and Shula is about to be firmly grounded in her new-found freedom."

Shula stared after Georgia, dumbfounded. Of all her friends, Georgia was the one she had thought would be open to understanding, or even just be intrigued by what Shula had said. She swallowed hard, forcing a cry back down that was threatening to overwhelm her, clearing her throat. She groped for her bag, got up, and walked stiffly out of the cafe.

Only later, when she was alone, did Shula allow herself to vent her pain and shock. She opened her Bible and re-read the passage again. And, as much as she tried, she could not shake nor change the understanding of what she had seen.

"Lord," she whispered. "Lord, am I wrong? Have I misunderstood? Surely Georgia would know. But she didn't seem to understand at all. Help me. Please help me Jesus."

My Lord immediately went to Shula. We stood there, He and I, and poured love all over her. Bending down, Yeshua whispered to Shula, "Do you trust me?"

"Yes, Lord. You know I trust you."

"Good. So, Shula, do you trust that Holy Spirit is able to stop you from going off in the wrong direction?"

"Yes, of course," she answered. "But people do, don't they? So often you hear of a famous tele-evangelist caught with another woman, or embezzling funds or something else. So, Lord, I have to be really careful, don't I?"

"Ahh, Shula. Let's talk about this," Yeshua said to her. "Yes, all those people do go off in the wrong direction, but tell me the answer to this. If your heart is soft to me, and you listen to me, do you really think I would let you go into danger? Could it be that I have warned and warned these people, and they haven't listened? They did what they wanted to do, not what I was asking them to do."

Shula sat and considered what the Lord had said to her. Slowly, we could see her putting the puzzle pieces together.

"Do you trust me, Shula?" He asked again.

"Yes, Lord, I trust you," she whispered.

Yeshua then gave her another piece of the puzzle. "I will not let your foot slip - I, who watches over you, will never sleep."

Grabbing her phone, Shula searched online for the verse and then looked for it in her Bible. "Psalm 121:3," her lips moved as she silently read the verse. "'I will not let your foot slip.' What does that actually mean?" And then went searching back through the concordance for the original meaning. *Foot slip, a shaking, wavering, tottering.'*

"Shula, am I trustworthy? Holy Spirit *will* keep you from going down the wrong path as long as your heart remains mine. I will not suffer your foot to be moved, which literally means when the shaking comes, I will not allow you to slip. Now Shula, do you trust me?"

It was like watching a flower go from being a tightly closed bud, to the unfurling into a full blossom. We watched Shula finally understand, that it didn't matter what anyone else said, if Yeshua said something to her, she could without question, entirely trust Him, and thus absolutely know that He would work it all out in her life.

But oh, such undoing and the cutting off of nebulous and incorrect beliefs. I knew it was going to be painful for her.

Like an apple tree
among the trees of the forest
is my lover
among the young men.
I delight to sit in his shade,
and his fruit is sweet
to my taste.
He has taken me
to the banquet hall,
and his banner over me
is love.
Strengthen me with raisins,
refresh me with apples,
for I am faint with love.
Song of Solomon 2:3 - 5

15

We were in our favourite place, Yeshua's Garden. Walking over the bridge, crossing the singing waters, with swathes of waving sunflowers bowing their heads before the King; just delightful. The bluebell woods beckoned to us singing charmingly with their little bells, and the coolness of the overhead canopy shed dappled light onto the flowers below. I knew where He was going. We were heading towards where He could watch the earth's sunrise and sunset - simultaneously, at the same time. A feat not easily achieved on earth, but here, in the place where time does not exist, the Creator can do whatever He wants.

We sat and watched as the earth spun slowly around on its axis and all the multitude of stars and planets rode the heavens. The sun and the moon bowed before Yeshua as they continued their daily dance of beauty.

We watched as the sun rose in one place and set in the other. Simultaneously. Beautifully coordinated dance in the heavens. As we followed the course of the sun, we saw that Shula sat outside on her deck and also enjoyed the sunset. Unbeknownst to her, Yeshua and I sat beside her. She had yet to understand that she lives in two places at the same time, for does not the Word say that those who are marked by Yeshua's blood are seated in Heavenly places? That is, at the same time as being on earth. No, Shula didn't know that yet, but she would learn.

Yeshua called His writing accoutrements to Himself. He could just speak and the letter would be written, but I knew that He loved to write these letters Himself, so that His fingerprints, His DNA would be all over His outpouring of love to Shula.

He started writing.

Dearest Shula,

I saw you watch the sunset I sent you tonight. I sat there with you and together we watched the glory of Heaven pulsing for that short time while I poured all my love for you into those glorious colours. Did you see the faint blushing pink? I chose that, for it mimicked your cheeks. As the sky grew darker, the crimson reflection of the sun on the clouds reflected the passion in my heart for you. It looked like fire in the clouds, and so it is, for I long for the time when your entire life is on fire for me.

How I long for you, Shula. Did you see the carpet of dark blue velvet gradually appearing as the stars lit up, just as your eyes light up when you are happy?

I long for you to know me intimately, Shula. For a relationship can only be properly founded on intimacy. And it is this heart-to-heart understanding and confidence in each other that I am longing to have with you; When your heart beats as one with mine.

My heart thumps in my chest at my longing for you.
My arms are open wide to gather you in
Align yourself with My passion,
resonate with My heart.
Live under My smile.

~~~ ❧ ♡ ☙ ~~~

Shula swung gently, back and forth on the deck swing, enjoying the cool evening as the last of the light dwindled into the evening sky. She felt vulnerable, extremely small but safe and protected. The magnificence of the sunset seemed to reach deep inside her heart and emotions, singing to her to look further and see the glory of God. There was something about sunrises and sunsets that brought an awareness of the presence of God, His unending greatness.

"Peace and promise, Lord,' she spoke softly. Her heart was a fragile thing, longing to be free, sensing its great love was about to come to her. "How flamboyantly beautiful, how unique is your artwork, Lord. It reaches right into me until I yearn to reach up into the sky and become one with you and your glory."

If she could only have seen with her spirit eyes, she would have seen Yeshua bursting with love and joy, for He had been longing, longing for so many seasons to hear those words.

"My Beloved," Yeshua said.

And, as if all of Heaven had heard, there was a sudden burst of praise for the Almighty.

"Let's now bring her into the place of oneness with me. She has neglected her own vineyard for long enough. Come into my garden, my sister, my bride. Come with me and gather the myrrh and spice. Let us eat honeycomb together and drink of the new wine."

The breeze and the flowers of earth obeyed the words of the Creator and blew a subtle scent over Shula, crowning her in the betrothal garland.

I have come
into my garden,
my sister, my bride;
I have gathered my myrrh
and with my spice
I have eaten
my honeycomb
and my honey;
I have drunk my wine
and my milk.

Song of Solomon 5:1

16

It was the warmth of love that Shula noticed. It reminded her constantly that she was never alone. The times of feeling forced to get up early because it was expected of her, fell off, and now getting up early to look at the sunrise, or just sit quietly was her daily sustenance. Often, she would know that Yeshua was there, very present, and sometimes she would feel His presence so clearly that she couldn't speak at all. Reading her Bible was no longer a chore. The words seemed to dance off the page.

Her life started to move in the same rhythm as Yeshua. As she tried to explain that to a friend, all she could find to say is, "I ask Him in the morning, 'Lord, what's on your heart today?' And I always know. I just know. Then what He has shown me, somehow fits into my day." She paused to reflect on what she had just said. "Well, actually, sometimes it's like that, and other times I feel an overwhelming need to really pray about it, but it's not like I used to. Not begging God, but more pouring my heart out for the person, or the situation." Twisting some hair around her finger, Shula reflected further. "Like, I'm intervening or advocating."

And then in the evening, Shula would sit and watch the sunset. "Father God, you are bragging again," and she would smile and think of His magnificence.

Through this time, I noticed how Yeshua would softly speak to her, drop words into her heart, and then the Spirits of Knowledge and Understanding would work with those words, explaining until Shula understood. Her heart truly was expanding.

Occasionally the concerns of the man-made systems would come up and she would revert to the old religious thoughts. The fear of displeasing God would rise up to strangle the new-found life out of her, so that she was in dread that the God who had power to damn her eternally would find her wanting and reject her.

She would start to panic, feeling that she had done something wrong and He had left her. It was then that the delightful presence of Yeshua would reassure her. For the Lord is endlessly patient, and He would again reiterate to Shula that He wants relationship with her, not religion.

As she grew in understanding of Yeshua, the sweetness of really deep intimacy, friendship and affection became her life's strength. I noticed that she was learning what the Lord had taught me, all those many years ago in Egypt, that to speak that which was not, as though it is, was hugely powerful. For Shula, it had begun with the unveiling to her of who she truly is. And even though she still hadn't grasped it, the smidgen of light was growing.

Shula had stopped praying. Let me hasten to say what I actually mean here. She had stopped trying to pray those tortuous long wordy prayers that did nothing but fill the emptiness with noise. She now prayed without ceasing. Her mind was filled with the delight of Yeshua, her heart constantly communicating with Him, even when she wasn't conscious of it. Praying that is, in truth and power, not the endless, ceaseless begging, but from the burgeoning understanding of who she was.

Her prayer life became less of an activity and an overwhelming condemnation, and more of a state of being. Shula was becoming the Bride she was always purposed to be.

Yeshua poured His heart out to Shula as she read her Bible, discovering new depths that had previously been hidden, but now her relationship with Him was becoming far more personal than she could ever have believed possible. A sense of destiny formed as a crown over her.

I saw. I saw when Yeshua placed that crown on her head.

I saw this. I knew that to rule and reign with Yeshua, Shula would have to undergo rigorous training. And it wouldn't be easy.

17

"THE WINTERS OF LIFE," Yeshua announced to the assembly. "Now is the time for the north winds to blow. For it is only as Shula experiences the cold seasons in her life, that she will grow. Just as it is necessary for the gardens on earth to have cold weather which destroys vermin, so it is necessary for Shula to go through this ordeal. Just as the cold builds resistance and stamina in plants, so it does in my people. It is the hard cold that allows the fruit to come. It is essential for setting the fruit in her life." He smiled and beckoned to Michael who had entered the room and stood at the back of the group.

Bowing low, Michael made his way to where Yeshua was standing. "My Lord, Lucifer is demanding audience with you."

"Yes, I've been expecting him. I will see him in the courts of justice."

Bowing again, Michael left to usher Lucifer into the courts, the place where he had been condemned all those eons ago. Ahh, such strategy my Lord uses.

Yeshua looked amused. I knew what was coming for over the many eons I had been with Him, I had learned of His ways and the ways of the Heavenly Kingdom; the formalities of the spiritual realms.

"I would like you all to come and bear witness to this moment." Yeshua and all the Angels instantly translated to the court room where He knew Lucifer would be waiting. Angrily waiting. For he had still not humbled himself to Almighty God.

Michael had some of his choice warriors with him, watching carefully. However, I knew that Lucifer would never be able to go anywhere in Heaven except where the Lord and His Father allowed. He was limited because of his own actions. Heaven had been closed to him for so very long.

Yeshua sat in the seat of Judgment.

He said nothing.

We simply sat and waited.

I looked at the ones who had followed us and was pleased to see the Living Letters and Shula's Timeline were also present. This was going to be good. Very good! The Angels appointed to Shula were also watching; those ones who constantly behold the face of the Father.

Yeshua waited. Lucifer waited. I knew who would break the silence first, and it wouldn't be Yeshua, for Lucifer was too impatient, too greedy, and so full of pride that he couldn't even for a tiny spot of earth time understand how he could not possibly win his proposed contest.

The garments he wore were a sad parody of his former glorious beauty. But he couldn't see it. He thought he was outshining even Yeshua. The stench of sin filled the judgment chamber. '*Oh Lucifer,*' I thought. '*I was pleased once to serve you, to be part of your glory. Now look at you. Pride is a dreadful thing. It completely destroys everything.*'

Of course, Yeshua knew what I was thinking, and He nodded slightly.

The contest of silence stretched and continued. I could hear a group outside the room break out into spontaneous praise, and as the beauty of it reached into the room, Lucifer's face twisted in anguish, for once it was he who led all of Heaven in worship. As the glory of God which rode on the praises wafted through the Chamber of Justice, Lucifer was forced to his knees.

But his pride asserted itself.

"Oh, great king," he said mockingly. "I see you have a particularly favoured one. One whom I will prove to you is false. She would come over to me, but you protect her too much." His arrogance was astounding, even to me who had once lived with it.

I could hear the Angels murmuring at Lucifer's audacity. But Yeshua just stared at Lucifer, unflinching, and completely in control.

"And what would you have me do, Lucifer?" Yeshua spoke very quietly.

If Lucifer wasn't so self-conceited, he would surely have recognised that tone.

"Oh, great one," he said mockingly to Yeshua. "Give me access to her. Let me show you her true character. Then we shall see who the more powerful one is. You, or me."

Oh, what provocation from the evil one!

But he should beware, because God who was and is and is yet to come, knows all things, is in all things and He knows Shula's heart better than Shula does herself. And he certainly knows everything there is to know about Lucifer and his plans and his ways.

And beware anyone who touches even a hair on His little ones' heads.

~~~ ❧ ♡ ☙ ~~~

Yeshua stood in the place where the four winds met. He raised both arms and called loudly, with great authority.

"Awake North Wind.
Come South Wind.
Blow on my Garden
May its fragrance be spread abroad."

The winds came at His command. They whipped His robes about, and blew His hair, tussling it playfully. The North Wind blew cold. Frost attached itself to Yeshua's beard. The brittleness of winter arrived coating everything in ice.

My heart sank, and even though I knew it was necessary that Shula go through this, it would be very painful. I could only pray for her.

Gradually the North Wind subsided and the South Wind started blowing gently, warmly, and the frost, ice and snow melted. Spring flowers started to bud and the grass grew, soft and green. Little brooks and streams flowed through the garden restoring all the new life.

"It is done," Yeshua said. "Come, Beryl. Now is the time for Shula to find out who she is."

He started to sing:

You are on a journey to know
the heart of the Father.
This journey will take you to mountain tops
and down into the deepest valley.
The journey will see your feet torn and bloodied
and your heart broken.
The road into the Father's heart is not easy
it's a path that will see you
misunderstood and maligned.
But this journey will see the glories
and riches and beauty of my Father
poured through your life.
You will see my radiance shining on your face
and the magnificence of my court
will be your dwelling place.
Who will follow this path?
Who will lose their life to gain eternity?
Who will follow me through the cross,
into the death of self and through to glory?
Who will follow the King?

18

As the sweetness of the summer fruits dwindled into the beauty of Autumn, Shula continued to grow more in love with Yeshua. She devoured the Song of Solomon, and could often hear the Lord speaking to her through the ancient words on the page, and see the symbolism even in one verse. She pondered 1:6 for a long time, wondering what meaning it could have for her.

> *"...made me take care of the vineyards,*
> *my own vineyard I have neglected."*

At night, as she lay in bed waiting for sleep to take her into the depths of rest, she would whisper from

Song of Solomon 3:2b, *"I will search for the one my heart loves. Jesus, I love you. I long to see you face to face."*

And she yearned to share this beauty and love she had found, her true heart's foundation. She would excitedly tell those in her church home group, her work colleagues, anyone who would listen. "It's Jesus, it's this Jesus. He is the answer, He is everything we have been looking for, and oh, how He loves us."

Sadly, I knew that Lucifer was just waiting. Planning and waiting to destroy her. That as Shula grew stronger, he would do everything within the scope that God had allowed, and destroy all that he could.

I could only pray for her, that as Yeshua had said so very long ago in the wonderful words of Luke 22:31,32:

> *"Simon, Simon, sa-tan has asked to sift each of you like wheat. But I have prayed for you, Simon, that your faith will not fail. And when you have turned back, strengthen your brothers."*

I knew that this test was unlike anything she would ever go through again. That anything the enemy of all of Heaven tried, was within the sphere that God had allowed. I could laugh, because while sa-tan might think he was hurting Shula, he was actually doing exactly what the Father required to be done. And that was to build a strong foundation in her life, steel for her spine and develop her weaponry skills. She was about to learn how to rule as the betrothed of Yeshua should.

"Shula, would you please come into my office?" Shula's boss called to her.

She stood up and went to the boss's office, wondering why she was being called. She tried to catch the eye of her friend, but her friend seemed to be engrossed in what she was doing.

"You want to see me?" she said, as she sat down.

The boss appeared awkward, fidgeting and clearing his throat. "Ahh, yes. Um. Ahem. Ah Shula, I have had some people mention that they are uncomfortable with all your God-bothering." He stopped speaking and reached for his cold coffee, giving himself time to think. "It's not that we don't respect you Shula, but I'm sorry, you mustn't bring God into the work place. It's not appropriate." He was obviously very stressed in delivering this message. The colour on his cheeks was high, and little beads of sweat pooled on his brow. "We can't have you pushing your God stuff everywhere, ok?"

Shula was stunned. She hadn't picked up this feedback from anyone. Everyone she had spoken to had appeared to be very interested, asking questions. "Who, exactly, is uncomfortable?" she asked.

"Yes, well. That's not important. Just some of the staff. So, I don't want you to talk about God stuff anymore, ok?"

"Lord!" Shula exclaimed loudly in her head. *"Help me."* And out loud she said, "So, you are discriminating against me on the grounds of religion?"

Her boss was starting to get annoyed. This wasn't going at all the way he had planned. He had always thought Shula was compliant and easily controlled. "Now, Shula. You know we have to allow freedom of speech, but some things you say border on hate speech. Right, are we done then?" He finished speaking and got out of his chair, signalling the meeting was over.

Nodding, Shula went back to her desk. Her friend seemed to be deeply engrossed in whatever she was doing.

Shula's heart was pounding. She felt that everyone was looking at her. Silently, she kept her communication open with her secret prayer language. And all afternoon, wondered who was so uncomfortable that they had said something to the boss. Who had she offended?

Driving home after work, Shula couldn't keep the hurt in, and her eyes started leaking. "Don't cry, don't cry, you can't see to drive if you cry." But it didn't make any difference. The pain that someone she had freely given of her heart to, had taken exception, and instead of saying something to Shula, had gone to the boss. It felt awfully like the air was being sucked out of the car. Her breathing was shallow showing the level of stress.

In his lair, sa-tan laughed. "Let's see what she does now," he said to his cohorts. "Let the pain of betrayal only just start to diminish and then we'll ramp it up to a stronger level." He chortled gleefully at the thought of the pain he would cause to Yeshua's beloved. And that, he knew, would kick the Son in his ever loving heart. "Oh, I'm so devious," he said to himself. "When I have finished with this SHULA," and he yelled her name, "She will curse him and come to me."

The demons and foul spirits around him joined in his malicious laughter.

~~~ ❧ ♡ ☙ ~~~

Shula kept to herself at work for the next week. Unable to understand what had happened, she was only professionally friendly and polite, did her work and went home again. It was with great relief that she greeted Sunday. "At least at church they talk the same talk as me, love Jesus, and love to talk about Him."

Georgia may not have understood, but she was her sister in the Lord. And sisters and brothers look out for each other. Sitting in her usual seat, Shula smiled at the people around her, enjoying the general chit chat and the buzz of the Sunday morning greetings. The musicians were doing their tuning of instruments and the atmosphere was generally very comfortable, relaxed. And Shula relaxed, ready to engage in the worship songs.

Her home group leader sat down beside her, on the edge of the chair, so he was obviously not going to stay. She greeted him warmly.

"Uh, Shula, can we have a quick chat after the meeting please?" His manner wasn't his normal welcoming committee style.

"Sure," she said. There was an unsettled feeling in her stomach. Something wasn't quite right. She pushed it away, telling herself she was just being silly, that she was still uptight about the work incident. He was probably going to ask her to make the supper or do a reading or something. And with that, she pushed it aside and turned her attention to joining in with the worship.

The home group leader found her after the service had finished, and led her to a corner where it was more private. Then the head Pastor joined them. Now Shula really started to wonder what was happening.

"Shula, you know how much we appreciate you. You have been part of this fellowship for a long time, and we have watched you grow. It has been such a pleasure. But recently, a few people have been concerned that you are going in the wrong direction. Georgia, and yes, she said we could say who it was, has come to us very worried that you have been caught up in something that is not scriptural and not right. That you are practicing mind-bending and mind-expanding principles." He paused, watching Shula's reaction carefully.

SHOCK!

Shula's body jolted in shock. She was not prepared for this. Never thought that her beloved church would not understand that it was Jesus whom she was running after.

"Tell us what is happening, Shula. We have men and women who are trained to deal with this sort of thing and I am sure they can help you get back on track. Mind-expansion is of course of the devil, and because you appear to be going down the wrong path, we ask that you step back from any and all services you are doing here at church and in home groups until we can resolve this."

So total was the consternation racing around Shula, that she couldn't think. Her mind was frozen. Her heart pounded, racing hard and she started to sweat. With difficulty she controlled her breathing.

"Did you want to tell us anything, Shula?" The Pastor spoke gently.

"I'm not doing any mind-expanding anything," she tried to explain. "I told Georgia that. I tried to tell her that Jesus and I are developing a really deep relationship and it feels as though it has expanded everything. That's what I said."

The Pastor looked concerned. "I wonder, Shula, if you have inadvertently strayed and been listening to a wrong spirit."

The demons sitting around listening to the conversation were beside themselves, laughing hysterically.

Numbly, Shula watched the Pastor and Home Group Leader walk away. How could this be happening? What was wrong? Maybe SHE was wrong. Maybe she had got it all wrong. Maybe, she needed to pull back and reassess what she had thought was Jesus.

Maybe, she *was* listening to evil spirits. She didn't even remember the drive home.

Shula felt numb. But numb was too mild a word to describe the coldness that held her. The agitation in her mind seemed to slip into her belly. She thought she was going to be sick.

Desperately, Shula knelt by her bed. "Lord, have I slipped into something evil? Forgive me, Jesus. Please cleanse me from this and set me free. I rebuke all evil in Jesus' name and renounce for believing your lies."

Fear and confusion swarmed around her.

Her Angels wept.

Sa-tan laughed.

Shula tried to pull right back from the closeness she had been finding in her relationship with Yeshua, believing she was wrong.

But it just didn't work. For, once you have experienced the love of Yeshua, there is no way back. I should know. I was so incomplete without Him that nothing I could do would separate me from His love. All my adventures in Heaven and on earth had cemented this firmly in me. Nothing can sever me from Him. And Shula was discovering this. She was inseparably, irrevocably tied to Yeshua. And nothing, absolutely NOTHING could ever disconnect her from Him again.

Much as she tried to disentangle herself from Him, Shula could not. It didn't matter how much she tried to fall back into her previous understanding of what it meant to be a 'good Christian,' her spirit soared at even His name being spoken or thought.

Over the next few days, Shula sought truth. And Truth was right there with her, teaching her that the only truth is found in relationship with Yeshua.

19

We watched Shula's journey falling in love with Yeshua, then her struggle to be free from man's opinion and approval.

The allegory of her odyssey to betrothal, and then to bride, had begun.

I saw her in the foothills of the mountain, where the growth is lush. It was there that Shula became the beloved, where in the chamber of verdant boughs and beams of cedar and rafters of firs, intimacy began, and Yeshua poured out His perfume on her. Where Angels wings extended over them, protecting them as she explored the heart and mind of her Lover, His depths and fathomless beauty.

And it was there that she was marked as His own.

But now, she had started to climb the mountain, for she must reach its pinnacle in order to find the valley on the other side. Shula had left behind the lushness and easy walking of the foothills. The path led her away from the abundance and shelter that the foothills offered. She now picked her way through the scrubby brush that offered little in the way of cover. It was not an easy climb.

But I knew there were two paths and she would have to choose.

As Shula carefully found her way over little stones, and then bigger ones, clambering over boulders, her faith grew, and we rejoiced.

20

"Lord, I don't understand all this. I have tried so hard to seek you. Now I am told that what I am doing is wrong, and that it's not you who I thought I was listening too, but outside influences. Help me, Jesus."

The pain of being misunderstood pelted her in her mind and heart. There was a constant theme running through her thoughts and it was that of, 'am I wrong?' But all it did was force her to seek Truth out even more.

Just as the Lord had known it would, what the enemy meant for evil, forced Shula to seek the Lord even more. She did much soul searching, asking herself, *'is there any truth in the accusations?'* Shula examined everything, double checked herself. We watched her as she went back into the Song of Solomon, reading it all very carefully, making notes, and finally coming to her conclusions.

"I'm not listening to the wrong voices, am I, Lord? I am hearing you, your heart and your love."

Exhausted from the emotional up and down, Shula's mind and body demanded rest. She could no longer stay awake, and even though it was the middle of a Saturday afternoon, she gave in and lay down, *'just for a while,'* she told herself. And fell asleep.

Shula dreamed.

In her dream she was standing in a field. It was a muddy field, for many people were walking, and running in a chaotic manner. In the dream, Shula saw herself speaking. As she spoke, she knew that the words spoken were words of life and they poured out of her mouth as beautiful pearls. But the pearls fell on the ground. The people were heedless of the riches that they were trampling into the mud. As she watched herself in the dream, Shula noticed one man. He was deliberately walking towards her, intent on what she was saying. As she continued to speak, she saw that one of the pearls coming out of her mouth was caught by the man. He held it in his hand, overawed at its lustre and beauty, and carefully put the pearl into his heart.

She woke up.

The dream was fresh in her memory. Taking every element of the dream, Shula examined it. Pearls coming out of her mouth as she spoke. 'Okay, that must be the Word of God,' she reasoned. But the words as pearls were being trampled underfoot. People were uncaring, not seeing what was right in front of them. Except for that one person.

"What does this mean, Lord?" And into her mind came the story Jesus had told of not casting pearls before swine. Gradually, pieces of understanding started to fit together like a jigsaw puzzle. Little glimmers of light broke through the dullness of pain, forcing apart the curtain of grief that had enveloped her for the last week. Images of her talking to people at work became superimposed over her dream and at last, she understood.

"I didn't use wisdom, did I, Lord? I was so excited that I didn't stop to think, and just threw my pearls of joy at anyone at all."

Yeshua clapped. He was so delighted that Shula understood His dream easily. "Did you see that, Beryl?" He asked me. And of course, I had seen it.

"The man," she said. "I was supposed to speak to him, not 'cast my pearls before swine.' So, I need to learn to listen to Holy Spirit's direction."

Shula sat on the bed twisting some hair around a finger, musing on the dream and the lessons in it. "Please forgive me, Jesus, for I did not listen to you, I listened to me."

She picked her Bible up and flicked it open to where she was currently reading. John 12. It was only as she read right through the chapter that understanding came - verse 49 said that Jesus only ever did or spoke what He heard and saw the Father doing and saying.

"Wow!" was all she could say. "I need to only do what you say, Lord. I brought all that pain on myself for no reason other than I didn't understand this. I was like a little child chatting away to anyone who stopped still for five minutes. And all it did was discredit you and wound me.

"But Lord, I cannot reconcile what the Pastor said with what I know. Now I feel afraid to go back to that church. Please show me. What is going on?"

A sudden breeze ruffled the pages of her Bible, and absently, Shula reached out to stop the pages creasing. She sighed, looking back down at her Bible, only to see the wind had turned the pages to the book of Hebrews. She just shrugged and started reading at chapter five. "I've never really understood Hebrews, Lord, so please show me what it means."

"Melchizedek," she muttered to herself. "A priest forever, a high priest. What does that even mean?" She continued reading to the end of the chapter, and as she read the last verse, stopped. Suddenly stopped. For there in the verse was the answer to her previous question about why her Pastor had completely missed what she was trying to tell him.

'But solid food is for the mature, who by constant use have trained themselves to distinguish good from evil.'

"Oh, Lord!" was all she could say.

Shula was starting to grow up. She had chosen the right path. It wasn't an easy path, in fact it was the hardest path, but it was the one that would ultimately lead her straight to Yeshua.

Awake North Wind
and come, South Wind!
Blow on my garden,
that its fragrance
may spread abroad.
Let my lover
come into his garden
and taste
its choice fruits.
Song of Solomon 4:16

21

Shula's love for Yeshua was so consuming that she looked for Him everywhere. If she woke in the middle of the night, her thoughts immediately flew to Him and her heart and mind were filled with praise, the longing of her heart filled with His nearness. In spite of the ruling of her Pastor and oversight, she refused to let go of Him. The beloved Lord with all He had shown her and drawn her into Himself, was so wonderful that she advised all who asked her why she no longer attended that church, to find Him for themselves. Most of her friends thought she was backsliding, quoting 'forsake not the gathering of yourselves together', but Shula knew, she was not forsaking anything, she was not backsliding. She was completely in love with Jesus.

Their responses varied. Many thought they already knew Jesus, but as Shula explained how they can have a much closer, deeper relationship with Him, some were curious. Others outright rejected what she was saying as error. They were happy in their secure little world.

Now, she no longer cared about their reactions, but prayed for them that their hearts and minds would be opened and they would see the glory and beauty available to all.

Over time, a few people had started to gather around her, joining her in her worship for the true King. His aroma filled her lounge room when they all came together in His name.

Though they couldn't see us, Yeshua, (and I because I was on His finger), came and soaked up their love and praise. The Angels joined in with Shula and her friends. Oh, how I longed for them all to see, so did some of those in their crowd of witnesses.

Yeshua's gift back to Shula was to pour even more of His love into her life.

And Lucifer, once known as the shining one, hated it. He again presented himself to Yeshua.

"You are still protecting her. If you are the Lord of Truth," he began.

And we knew that Lucifer was again challenging the Lord of All, just as he had all those eons ago.

"If you are the Lord of Truth, then allow me more access to her. THEN we shall see if she is as you say." He smirked, confident of his ability to destroy and corrupt the Lord's Betrothed.

I could see Michael's hand gripping his sword tightly. 'Not yet, Michael,' I silently said to him. And yes, in our realm, thought is conversation. I knew that Yeshua had also heard Michael's inner anger. He held His hand up, stopping any confrontation.

If Lucifer had any type of understanding at all, he would have caught the glint in Yeshua's eye. *'Oh, he's in trouble now,'* I thought in glee. *'How can Lucifer possibly think that he will be able to destroy the Lord's Beloved?'*

"What is your proposal, Lucifer?" The King of all Kings asked the evil one.

As he laid out his planned agenda, I alone could feel the anger coursing through Yeshua. But oh! I knew! This would not end well for Lucifer.

"I agree with your proposal, Lucifer. But be warned! My Beloved will crush your head."

The interview was over.

Lucifer disappeared back to work his evil.

Yeshua and I went to His garden, that place of great peace and beauty. The place where He and Shula often sat together.

22

The time of Lucifer's hatred to be poured out had come.

Shula's Timeline wept with the knowledge of what was to come.

~~~ ⋘ ♡ ⋙ ~~~

Humming to herself, Shula took her time in the grocery store selecting what she needed and putting it in her cart. The understanding of what had happened and how she had contributed to it, now filled her with peace. She had won the victory over what sa-tan had meant for evil, and grown through the pain.

A great burst of joy bubbled from her Spirit, finding its way out in a giggle. She quickly grabbed her phone pretending she was laughing at something on there, which made her laugh even more at her own silliness. Inside, she felt that she was fizzing as delight grew, and imagined people's reactions if she erupted in a shout of victory, jumping while doing a high five, just like a cartoon character. 'Would I do it in the cleaning products aisle or by the frozen peas?' she thought, her eyes dancing in delight at the thought. As her heart poured out thanks and praise for the understanding of how she had contributed to the discipline at work, and how her Pastor was struggling through issues of his own, she suddenly saw another facet of it, and forgave herself. *Forgiveness by the fruit n veggies,'* She thought. *'How apt. Fruit of the Spirit.'*

Victorious joy emanated out from her and all the Angels in the store caught it, shouting their praises to God.

The ripples of joy edged out, circles of influence widening, each ripple bumping into the other and pushing the hope generated by joy further out until the entire store was covered. Joy fell on a man who started whistling, and that doubled the amount of joy around him, which then bounced into someone else walking by.

All those who walked past Shula were influenced, her brilliant smile landing in their hearts and infecting them. Joy was contagious that day.

"Mankind have no idea of who they are, do they, nor the power latent in them?" I said to Yeshua.

"No, they have no idea that once they are in me, they are elohim." He responded. "But Shula is finding out."

Sa-tan also saw this and raged in anger as his plans to divert Shula from her destiny were being thwarted. "Next on our plan. Act on it, NOW!" he roared as the demons and spiteful ones scrambled to obey.

As she made her way to her car to put her groceries in the back, Shula was still smiling. Her heart was full of praise for all that God had done for her. *'Nothing, but nothing can separate me from the love of God.'* This verse was running through her mind. She opened the car with the alarm fob, listening to the beep indicating it had been unlocked, and walked around the back of the ...

What?

She checked. Yes, that was her car. But she didn't leave it like that. How?

Bewildered, Shula looked around, trying to find anyone who could explain the huge dent in the back of her car and the writing scrawled on the damage. Her scalp tightened and crawled with tension, as her throat tried to refuse to breathe.

Interlaced with expletives and in poorly written language was a message:

DI **** BITCH

Unable to comprehend what she was seeing, Shula looked around to see if anyone had also seen it, but there was no one in the parking lot. The rear of her car was pushed right in, and then the horrible message spray-painted in fluorescent orange over the dent.

We waited to see what Shula's reaction would be. Her Angels looked grim, and we watched the evil ones dancing in delight at hurting this precious one of the Lord.

Shula pulled her phone out and dialled emergency. Many hours later. after the police had been, her insurance company notified, and her car towed away, Shula was finally able to get home, by bus. Her insurance policy did not have provision for a rental car.

Unlocking the door to the house, Shula just dumped her groceries in the kitchen. She put the kettle on and wandered into the lounge room, where she sank into a chair, and started crying.

"Lord, who would do that? Why would they do that? It's not the dent, it's them going without leaving anything to say who they were, or sorry or anything. And to paint *that* on my car? Why?"

The logistics of the next few weeks raced around her brain, faster, wider tracks, spinning off into other thoughts and coming back again to *why*?

The cat bunted her legs bringing her into the present. The kettle had boiled. She was tired, the cat was hungry and the groceries needed to be put away. "Right, first things first, cat to be fed, cup of coffee to be made and groceries put away. Then I can sit down and try to work through this."

Later, after feeding herself just a piece of toast and a banana, Shula allowed her mind to go back over the happenings of the day, tears trickling down her face. But there was no peace in that, so she picked her Bible up, opening to John that she was slowly working her way through. She smiled at all the underlining in it. John was full of good things. John 16 she read. Lips moving, quietly reading, often going back and reading a verse again, she read verse 33: "I have told you these things, so that in me you may have peace. In this world you will have trouble. But take heart! I have overcome the world."

"Right there. Jesus," she said stabbing at the verse with her finger. "That's why I love you. For in this horrible day, you are affirming who I am in you, and guiding me back to your heart. I will not fear, for what can man do to me."

For the next two weeks while her car was being mended, Shula had to catch the bus to and from work, and it was exhausting, for while driving her car only took her twenty minutes, she had to walk ten minutes to the bus stop, and then the bus route wound around every street, stopped often, arriving some distance from her work, where she had another fifteen-minute walk. In all, her normal twenty-minute journey stretched out to over an hour. She had to leave home earlier and arrived back much later. By the time Friday rolled around, Shula was tired. Very tired. At the end of the following week, her defences were lowered through fatigue and she knew it was starting to show in her work. The repair shop had told her they were having difficulty sourcing a part which put the return of her car out for another week. There was no way for her to go out anywhere except by bus, and the bus didn't run very frequently on the weekend. The police hadn't found who had tagged her car, and she lived with the feeling of constantly looking over her shoulder to see who wanted her dead.

Her weekly grocery shop became an act of her will, for the bus didn't go directly to the mall. Two buses. A long time. Then carrying it all home again. Tired, so tired. She mocked herself, for weren't people doing this sort of thing all the time? Why did she think she would be exempt from this?

Then there were the new neighbours and their parties. After a noisy Friday night, she decided to talk to them and ask if they could keep the noise down after midnight. Their response was horrible, full of curses and swearing, and the next morning when she went outside, she found the house had been egged.

Standing there, staring at the broken eggs, yolk hardening by the morning sun, Shula began to crack, just as the eggs had. Little crack, crack, crack of her composure. Stress, and insufficient sleep and rest took its toll on her. She stumbled into the house, before allowing herself to cry, wail loudly.

And the demons laughed.

Yeshua was angry. The Angels could only watch.

It has been said that crying relieves tension but it is also exhausting, and Shula fell asleep in utter weariness, the crying further depleting her reserves, but allowing expression of pain.

She stayed inside for the rest of the day, and all Sunday, only going outside on Monday morning to do the same thing all over again, walk to the bus, catch the bus that took forever and then deposit her a long way from work, where she walked again, getting caught in the rain, arriving at work late and wet.

Her boss was not pleased. There was a feeling of not being able to please him, no matter how hard she tried. A few people had been laid off recently. The company wasn't doing well. Shula had to keep her job. She couldn't afford not to, so kept to herself, working even harder.

Finally. Friday arrived. Surely her car would be ready, and anyway, she was absolutely ready for the weekend, for a rest. Hopefully she would be able to catch up with friends and have a time of praise and communion with them. Refreshing, renewal.

By three o'clock, she hadn't heard from the panel-beaters so called them, only to be told that her car had been ready to pick up since yesterday. Oh, that was frustrating. "I'll just check with my boss to see if I can get off work early and come and get it," she said to the person on the phone.

"Dave," Shula knocked on her boss's door.

He looked up. She saw how grey he looked, harried and anxious. "Are you okay, Dave?"

"Come in, Shula. Shut the door, please. Take a seat." He gestured at the chair.

Immediately, Shula's anxiety levels rose, remembering the last time she had been in this seat. Had someone complained again? But she hadn't said anything.

"You know the company hasn't been going well. You know we have had to make people redundant. I'm so sorry, Shula. I have to make you redundant, too." He handed her an envelope. "Your final pay, together with any holiday pay owing and your bonus will be in your account tonight. This is the breakdown of it all and also a reference, which is from me, not the company." He looked defeated. "Come on, I'll help you pack your desk up. You may as well go now instead of waiting until five."

Dave led the way out of his office with Shula stumbling after him, unable to believe what was happening. Misunderstood by someone she had thought was a good friend. Betrayed by a work colleague, abandoned by her church, threatened by who knows who, and her car crunched into. And now this. No job.

Shula swallowed, swallowed again, desperate to keep control of her emotions, taking shaky breaths as she put her things into the box Dave had found.

Somehow, she had phoned for a taxi to get her to the garage where her car had been ready since yesterday. Somehow, she drove herself home. And somehow, she had made it inside without completely collapsing.

Standing in the middle of her bedroom, her trembling insides welled up, chattering her teeth and pushing against her lungs. Unable to breathe. Heart fluttering. Shula crumpled as though someone had kicked her legs out from under her.

"Lord," was all she could say. Even in the extreme pain, she reached for her only secure place, Yeshua.

As she processed the shock, Shula got angry. And the Lord was ready for it. He who is so wise, so loving, so kind. As Shula raged at Him, lashed out in her pain and confusion, yelling and screaming, He stood as she hit against Him, absorbing her blows, just as He had all that time before on the cross of death.

We, I on Yeshua's finger, and all the Angels in Heaven, had all witnessed the distress of Yeshua's disciples as He was hung on that hateful cross, hung neither on earth nor in Heaven. The distress and disbelief as all they had thought was going to happen dissipated in front of them. Not understanding that this was the moment of their greatest victory.

But we knew. They were only seeing a very small part, and so it was with Shula. In her distress, she thought that all she had believed, was built on nothing.

Yeshua looked at me. "We are needed in the Hall of Judgment."

I have ceased being amazed at travel in Heaven. It is instant. Whereas on earth, it can be wearying, long distances measured by how far a man can walk.

As always, Yeshua stood by the Judgment Seat. Michael and the mighty ones formed a circle around Lucifer.

"I have come for my reward, Yeshua," Lucifer boasted. "Shula will no longer worship you. She will follow me. You may as well hand me my crown now."

A guttural growl came from Michael. The mighty warriors with him tensed, swords ready.

Yeshua smiled, and then throwing His head back, started laughing. It was not a laugh of amusement. It was frightening. It was a laugh of savage victory and Lucifer was about to understand how incompetently he had read his position.

Holding His hand up, His laughter stopping abruptly, Yeshua looked so angry. Righteous justice and anger. "The contest is not over, Lucifer. You have badly misjudged the situation. Shula and I have one last conversation before Justice is served."

He swiped time and distance away and we all watched.

"You promised, you promised you would never leave me. You promised you would always protect and provide for me. Now look. I have no job. I have been disowned and abandoned. I have been betrayed and potentially, now I could be homeless as I have no job, no money. You promised. You are a liar. A liar. You are vengeful and spiteful. And I want nothing to do with you." Shula yelled her pain at the One she loved.

'Snicker, snicker, snicker,' Lucifer chuckled at that.

Yeshua glared at him. "Be quiet Lucifer. You understand nothing."

We all waited in silence. The Fear of God saturated the atmosphere.

Shula finished her vitriolic onslaught and sat dejectedly, hiccupping. Weeping. Was there nothing and no one she could trust?

"Have you finished?" Yeshua asked her, calmly.

"Yes!" Shula was not going to show any weakness to Almighty God. She was so angry.

"Tell me, Shula. Have you had something to eat today?"

"Yes!"

"Good," He responded. "So, do you have somewhere to sleep tonight?"

"Yes!" Shula did not like where this questioning was going. It was about to unveil her faulty belief.

"Shula, do you have clothes on?"

"YOU KNOW I DO!" she shouted at Him.

"Excellent. You have everything I promised you, Shula. I have done exactly as I promised. You have all you need for today. I have only ever promised you provision for today. I have never promised you tomorrow."

Absolute silence filled Creation and Heaven.

Shula sat completely still as she listened to the Lord of All declare that He was King, He was definitely, unquestionably, and undeniably sovereign.

We could see revelation unfold over Shula, that This Yeshua, this King, could not and never would lie, and would never abandon His precious one.

Slowly, as she processed what He had said, we could see light glimmering, breaking open false beliefs and destroying them. She just had to trust Him. That no matter what the circumstances, He was God. She was not.

She knelt on her bedroom floor, in the glory of God,

"Lord," was all she said. Her heart knelt. Her mind knelt. And in that one word, at that point, Shula became Betrothed to the King of all Kings.

Lucifer left. He had lost.

23

All the while Shula had been struggling in earth's realm, she didn't realise the progress she was making. We had watched from Heaven's perspective as she climbed the precipitous mountain face, with the many dangers the journey carried.

From the place of lush vegetation where Shula first encountered the Lord, and from there started to explore the depths of His love. A place that she longed to stay in, but the Lord led her up the mountain.

Shula did not know that the mountainous terrain held the place of the greatest growth, with the sparsest vegetation, unaccompanied by anyone, for she only, could make this journey. No one could make it for her.

We had watched as she eagerly followed the Lord out of the foothills into the lower reaches of the mountain.

And we watched as she started to struggle through the loose scree. We watched as the boulders started to tumble around her, and watched her reaction. But when the mountain top was within sight, a short climb away, that was then the most dangerous place; the place where the enemy unloosed as many boulders as he could.

It had threatened to take Shula down. All the enemy plans to unseat her love for Yeshua pounded around her like the mountainous boulders. But her heart was soft before the Lord, and even though in her pain she had cried aloud, just as King David had many times, she refused to let go.

The climb grew harder, drawing on all her reserves and determination. Dropping to her knees, she came to the end of herself. Yeshua knelt beside her on the rough terrain, encouraging her to get up again, keep going.

Wearily, she got to her feet. The climb had exhausted her, drained her energy. Refocusing her sights on her Lord, she grimly held onto His presence and continued the final ascent, the steepest, most dangerous part of the climb.

We watched, as at times, Yeshua carried Shula, supporting her, going ahead and calling her closer to Himself.

Then finally.

Finally, she was on the mountain top. The peak.

She dropped to her knees, utterly spent, kneeling before the Lord.

If she could only see herself now, she would see that He was binding up what had been torn.

Two Angels went to Shula and dressed her in a new gown. It was the colour of the pale morning sky and had stars sown around the hem. The Angels stepped back and bowed. Yeshua came to meet Shula. Then Yeshua placed a crown on her head. They stood together on the mountain peak.

All the pain that Shula had felt, drained away. Her bedroom was filled with the essence of hope. There was a new understanding that had built strength in her mind and spirit. She closed her eyes and raised her hands to worship the great Creator.

Yeshua opened her Spirit eyes and showed her where she was standing. She faced Him, He whom her soul loved, He who had rescued her and healed her. He, who had chosen her. He reached His arms out and gathered her to Himself, holding her until she felt her bones would turn to rivers and flow into Him.

He planted His standard, right there on the mountain top. The proclamation that He had gained this territory, that He ruled here. The flag unfurled, showing the brilliance of the rainbow before the Throne, blazing the proclamation THIS ONE IS MINE.

They stayed there all night. Yeshua kindled a fire and the light flickered across her face as she looked up into the night sky at the stars who bowed before the Lord, and sang their songs of love to Him.

Something major had shifted in her perception of who Yeshua was and who she was.

He showed her His promises, and they opened out before her as she looked through space and time.

Only as the rosy fingered dawn brushed tendrils of sleep aside and lit on Shula's cheeks, did the night-time dreaming end. Shula yawned and stretched, yearning to get back to the place where she and Yeshua had been.

"A dream, it was a dream. But maybe it was actually a vision of the night just as Job said." She yawned again and tossed the bedclothes off, ready to start her day.

The crushing bewilderment and pain of yesterday had gone, replaced with the certainty that her Lord was with her and she had no cause to fear.

We, watching from the other realm saw that Shula had started her descent from the pinnacle, down to the valley laid out before her.

Your head crowns you
like Mount Carmel,
Your hair
is like royal tapestry;
the king is held captive
by its tresses
How beautiful you are
and how pleased,
O love,
with your delights.
Song of Solomon 7: 5-6

24

Dearest Shula,

I will never leave you, Shula. Through all, from beginning to end, and all that earth's life will throw at you, I promise, I will never leave. You will never walk alone.

See? Look how the fetters have been falling off you. See how your freedom is becoming reality.

Shula, you will face many challenges and trials throughout your life on earth. This is the time of training, for you are destined to rule and reign with me. Many will fall away because they refuse to enter the training ground.

The training ground, as you know, can be very painful. Many more will remain as babies instead of embracing my discipline. They will not be able to reign as they are destined to, for you cannot have an immature ruler.

My church has been taught that because they are in me, their life will become easier, and some even teach how to be financially free, and when the adversities in life afflict them, they cannot stand, for they have not been taught to withstand the evil one, nor even the world's brokenness.

You have stood under such great pressure, and I am proud of you, Shula. Do not think that these are all the trials and troubles you will face in life, but you are learning how to deal with them - in humility and love.

No matter what the enemy throws at you, remember this, My Father dwells in the praises of His people. So, where there is heaviness, sing your praises, and all Heaven will join in. Think about it like this; When the enemy onslaught is pouring his evil heaviness on you, if you will but sing your praises, my Father has promised to sit in the midst of those praises, and because He is there, the evil one cannot stand against you.

I will teach you how to use your weapons of warfare, Shula. You cannot rule with me if you are not equipped. You cannot reign if you stay in the safety of the nursery.

Shula, trust me. Trust what I show you. As long as your heart is soft to me, and you feast your eyes on me, I have promised to keep you, so your feet will not stumble, your eyes will always know my Truth.

I am always here Shula, and I am teaching you.

With all the love there is, and that is me, my Father and Holy Spirit, for we are LOVE,

Yeshua.

He kissed me and pressed me as His covenant seal on the letter.

Sixty queens there may be,
and eighty concubines
and virgins beyond number;
but my dove, my perfect one,
is unique;
the only daughter of her mother
the favourite
of the one who bore her
The maidens saw her
and called her blessed;
the queens and concubines
praised her
Who is this
that appears like the dawn?
Fair as the moon,
bright as the sun,
majestic as the stars in
procession?
Song of Solomon 6:8 - 10

25

Shula didn't want to leave the mountain peak, the place where the presence of Jesus was so real, so tangible. The place where her heart had finally acquiesced that He was Lord, that there is none other besides Him.

But she couldn't live on the top of the mountain, where the air was thin and very little grew. The climb down the mountain to where she could see far below her into the valley, would be tortuous.

As Shula began climbing down the mountain, she slipped and slid in the loose shingle, sometimes causing her to lose her foothold, sa-tan looked on, furiously angry at his prize escaping his grasp.

Unseen by Shula, with nothing but malice seeking the end of this incredible threat to his kingdom of destruction, the enemy devised a plan and despatched one of his demons to carry it out. The demon came up behind her, and pushed her, intending for her to tumble down, off the mountain and to her death. While he had lost her to the Kingdom of Light, if she died, she would do no further harm to his evil.

But sa-tan had overstepped the boundaries the Lord had placed. He acted illegally.

Shula's Angel caught her. While her new gown was torn and dirty, and she was scratched and bleeding, she was shaken, but not seriously hurt.

Sitting on a boulder, calming herself enough to continue the descent, into her heart came a scripture: *'In everything give thanks, for this is the will of God in Jesus concerning you.'* Still sore from the tumble, Shula rubbed her elbow and started to give thanks. Feebly at first, and then more convincingly. Wiping the trickles of blood coming from numerous scrapes, grazes and scratches, she sang her thanks.

As Shula offered her thanks, at first whispered into the air, the up-drafts caught it, and we saw it start to rise; praise as incense joined with feeble thanks. We sang with her, lending our voices to hers.

A calmness came over her. We knew it was the presence of the Lord as He opened His gates, just as He had promised He would do with the sacrifice of thanks. Energised, Shula stood up and started her journey again, down the mountain, praises to God pouring out of her.

We watched as Shula's thanks opened more gates. As yet, she was not able to see the different realms as they worked together; how her thanks opened gates both in the spiritual and the physical realms. For as she gave thanks to God in earth's realm, He opened the way, a gate, for a new job. And thus, her journey continued, her thanks, a new job, the Lord's provision for her, and her growth as she learned the ways of the Kingdom.

Pausing to look at the glorious view, the sound of sobbing caught Shula's attention. She listened intently. A little off the path, to her left, knelt some women. After watching for a moment, Shula carefully picked her way over to them.

"Why are you crying? Why aren't you on the path?" Questions flowed through her mind and out of her mouth. "What are you doing up here?"

One of the women wailed louder. "We were promised the truth. We were told of great riches up here. He said if we would do everything his way, we would be safe. If we just followed along, he would give us everything we wanted. And we only wanted to live in peace and prosperity, so we did as he said."

"We have always lived here," another said.

And many voices joined in, all calling out their story. Clamour, clamour, clamour. A cacophony of misery.

"Who? Who said it? Who is 'he'?" Shula questioned them.

"He did," Another woman cried, pointing over to her left.

The Lord opened Shula's eyes. On the side of the mountain were many, many, many people. All held captive. She saw the enemy camped around these people. But what was strange, was that all the people had to do was to stand up, and walk out of their prison, for there were no bars, and the guards were in turn being held at bay by Angels.

There were Angels everywhere, exhorting the people to get up, to start singing praises to God. But most didn't listen, or complained it was too hard, it was easier to just stay where they were. It was easier to whine and complain, than actually follow what God had laid out for them in His Word.

"Listen to me," Shula called out as loudly as she could. "Listen. This prison you are in is not real. If you will simply determine to stand up, and start to praise God, He will ensure your freedom."

The majority of the people murmured at her words. A few started to stand up but were pulled back down by those they were sitting with.

Shula tried again. "Put on the garment of praise for the spirit of heaviness. I'll sing with you. I'll help you."

She started to sing praises to her Lord. For Shula who had fought through her own captivity, could see it so easily, and her thankful heart rose in praise to Almighty God. A few of the people gained courage from Shula and while their voices were feeble, hoarse from lack of use, they started to praise, first as a whisper, then like a rust-ridden gate creaking open. Their Angels picked up the praise and joined in. For no Angel of God can resist the joy of singing to the Lord.

All over the encampment, people were at first startled, then encouraged. Among every group, a few more stood up and engaged in the songs of praise.

Yeshua was dancing with delight. The more the people praised Him, the more powerful His dance.

I looked down at the movements His feet were making in His dance, and I saw He was dancing on the head of the enemy. As the people praised louder and stronger, His dance grew more intense. It reminded me of Moses all that time ago, that while he sat on the boulder and held his hands up, Israel prevailed. It was Moses' act of praise and worship to God that broke the enemy's power. And so, today, the act of praise was breaking the enemy's power over these people.

As she saw the people being set free, Shula's jubilation increased, shouting wild ululations of victory. The mountainside rang with triumph.

But her time here was finished. She had done what she could, and now Yeshua wanted Shula to follow Him further down the mountain. Seeing Jesus beckoning her on, Shula hesitated, uncertain. "But Lord, shouldn't I stay and help these people? I can't leave them here."

"Shula, you have done all I wanted you to do, now it is time for you to continue your journey, and I will take care of these people. I have already appointed the right person to do so."

She wasn't convinced. "But if I leave them, they will fall back into their captivity. I should stay with them."

Yeshua looked sombre. "You have a choice, Shula. I will never demand that you do anything. Follow me, or stay here on the mountainside."

Once again, the two paths appeared at Shula's feet. One went down the mountainside, and the other veered off to where the people were.

Pride jostled with humility.

Pride reared its head and spoke to Shula. "These are your people. You deserve for them to follow you. After all, you brought them out of their captivity."

Shula's eyes flashed in pride at the thought of what she had done; rescuing all these people from the enemy's camp. She should be the one they followed.

Quietly, humility bowed before Yeshua.

Nothing else was done or said. Shula had to make the decision.

She looked at the people. She looked at the path. And she remembered the mountain peak experience. He whom her heart desired above all. She started to quote a passage she had learned from The Song.

"His cheeks are as a bed of spices, as sweet flowers: his lips like lilies, dropping sweet smelling myrrh. His hands are as gold rings set with the beryl:

his belly is as bright ivory overlaid with sapphires. Where has your lover gone, most beautiful of women?

Which way did your lover turn?"

Giving the people a last look, Shula once again started to follow Yeshua.

We rejoiced. She had followed her Lover and put her pride and her own desires under her feet.

The difficult and perilous descent became somewhat easier, and Shula noticed small scrub growing, while the boulders weren't as large. It was easier to breathe here; the air wasn't as thin. Shula began to think that she had conquered all there was to subdue, and let her gaze waver from Yeshua.

Instantly, sa-tan made his move. A heaviness like a suffocating garment folded itself over Shula.

It became difficult for her to move. Breathing felt as though it took too much effort. Her legs started dragging, as thoughts of defeat kept shuttling around her mind.

Darts from the enemy were hurled constantly. Thoughts of *'You won't make it.' 'Who do you think you are?' 'You are useless, do you really think you could be victorious?' 'The church was right, you are wrong.' 'Your boss was right to fire you, you were useless.'*

The more Shula fought the attack off, the more the bombardment increased.

The thoughts came in increasing volume and viciousness: 'kill yourself, end this misery.' The enemy tried his tactics as he had back in the supermarket car park with the death wish, and further up the side of the mountain when he had tried to push her off to her death. All his evil ploy leading to Shula being taken out as a threat to his dark kingdom.

"Lord, help me," at last she cried, desperately. "Jesus, help me!" Shula called out again, for it felt that she was barely containing her sanity.

And just as He did when Peter started to drown all those long years before, Yeshua was right by Shula holding her tight.

"Put on the garment of praise for the spirit of heaviness," He said. "Use my name, Shula. And the power of my blood."

Nodding, Shula did as Yeshua said.

"In the name of Jesus, I command this spirit of heaviness to leave now."

She stood and waited for it to obey. Maybe just a tiny bit had lifted.

"In the name of Jesus, I bring the blood of Jesus against this heaviness. Lord, cover me, over, under, around me. All over me Jesus."

The Blood always responds, and as Shula started to use her weapons of warfare, the enemy stopped mid-sentence as he uttered curses and thoughts into Shula's mind.

The Blood descended, covering Shula, every atom of her body being drenched in its redemption.

Resonating with power that sang into Shula's mind, freeing it from the tyranny of torment, the Blood then coiled and sprang out at the enemy, inflicting injury until the enemy ran.

Smiling in satisfaction, Yeshua held His sword up, and the enemy was forced to flee. "Don't stop, Shula," He said, "Learn to live under my Blood."

She sat on a rock. Down below the landscape appeared both alternatively frightening, while at the same time, beckoning. But she was exhausted. Pulling her knees up to her chest, she encircled them with her arms; perhaps a protective measure. But Shula didn't know if she could go on. It all seemed so difficult. Emotionally fraught with danger on all sides.

She looked around to see if there was any way she could go back, without back-tracking, to the top of the mountain to only go down the other side.

Then she thought of the people who were just stuck there. Stuck going neither forward nor back because they were either too scared, or didn't know Jesus, or had believed lies. Or even, that they felt safe sitting there, because it was comfortable.

And then she thought of the love, the intimacy shared with Jesus, how He was the one constant in her life. Regardless of how painful and difficult times were, He had been there. And He had also joined in the wonderful, joyful moments as well.

No. She couldn't stay here. She had to move on, keep going forward and search for Him. *'For it was only when I will be with Him, face to face,'* she decided, *'that I will be satisfied. Nothing else compares, nothing matters.'*

Daring only to put one foot in front of the other, Shula started down the steep gradient again. "Lord, I trust in you. I trust you to keep me safe," she called out to the wind, the emptiness of the mountain side.

Oh, but Yeshua and I were there. She didn't see us, but my Lord never left her side at all.

Slipping, often sliding in the loose dirt, and stumbling over stones on the path, Shula made her way down to where the vegetation grew thicker. Little scrubby bushes clawed at her legs, ripping her gown further.

Gradually, the steep sides of the mountain eased out to gentle slopes, and still, Yeshua led Shula on. Through the scrub, over rocks, and into a dark, forbidding forest where very little light found its way to the forest floor.

Standing very still, her senses on alert, like an animal sniffing and listening for danger, this forest felt foreboding. It felt dark. There was a path, but it wasn't well used, as not many had followed Yeshua this way.

Stumbling and tripping over fallen branches, rocks and loose scree, Shula went towards the sound of running water. She was thirsty, so very thirsty. Following Yeshua had taken everything she had, and now, she had nothing left, no more reserves, nothing further to give. Yet her love for her Lord drove her beyond exhaustion, forcing her body to obey her spirit.

Little patches of sunlight became more frequent, with the sound of water growing louder. She forced her utterly drained legs to walk towards where she could see light and hear the water.

Finally, breaking through the darkness of the forest and into a grassy clearing. Running water, clean fresh water. Warm sunlight, peace.

And Shula sagged, her legs collapsed under her. She lay on the ground. Her race was run. It was over.

She slept, the sleep of extreme tiredness.

Yeshua watched over her, whispering His love. "Remember," Yeshua whispered, and the South wind picked it up and blew it over Shula, like Autumn leaves scattering before the four winds. "Remember" swirled around her, covering her like a blanket.

May the wine
go straight to my lover,
flowing gently over lips and teeth
I belong to my lover,
and his desire is for me.
Come, my lover,
let us go to the countryside,
let us spend the night
in the villages.
Let us go early to the vineyards
to see if the vines have budded
if their blossoms have opened
and if the pomegranates
are in bloom —
there I will give you my love.
The mandrakes send out their
fragrance and at our door
is every delicacy both new and old
that I have stored up for you,
my lover.
Song of Solomon 7:9-13

26

Yeshua loved the aroma of Shula's perfume, the perfume of her love for Him. He is so tender to His love. It made my heart ache and remember the longing when I was separated from them.

As He sat by the stream, Yeshua sang,

"I will no longer, I can no longer, deny Myself;
I will sweep you off your feet,
I will romance My beloved.
The time of dreaming and the longing of my heart
is now fulfilled.
This is a time of laughing."

I looked at Shula's torn and dirty clothing. She had scratches, bruises and grazes all over her. And yet, she had continued on in her journey, often crawling, barely able to move, to be with her Lord. Now, now He was honouring her, loving her and watching over her as she rested.

Shula groaned, the pain of the multitude of abrasions and contusions dragging her back to wakefulness. Struggling to her feet, she looked around. She was in a secluded glen. The cedars and fir trees formed a semicircle around the grassy area, with their boughs making a canopy of rafters. Then she saw Yeshua.

"Lord," the word whispered as a sigh. Through her extreme tiredness, she still tried to stand, to go to Him, expending the last of her strength. "I'm sorry," was all she could say, and started to crumple to the ground.

Yeshua caught her and carried her to a table spread with all the food of Heaven, feeding her Himself until she started to gain strength, and then carried her to the stream, where the crystal waters washed over her, Yeshua holding her up, tending to every cut, bruise, abrasion, and scratch.

I smiled. For I was on that hand that so very gently scooped up the living waters which healed every part of Shula. Her gown, torn, dirty, stained from her life's journey, became shining white.

New life infused itself through her, instantly healing and changing her, closer to the image of Yeshua.

My Lord looked at His betrothed. All the love present in that man who is God, shone on her.

"How beautiful you are, my darling! There is no flaw found in you. Come with me, away from the lions' dens, the mountain haunts of the leopards. You have stolen my heart, my sister, my bride. How delightful is your love, and the fragrance of your perfume more than any spice. You are a garden fountain, a well of flowing water. Come home with me."

Shula looked at her reflection in the still waters. Her gown! Woven from rainbows and edged in angels' wings. Tears crushed in great pain formed diamonds scattered among the rainbows. It was beautiful. She was beautiful. Her love had found her, taken her from the before life and now this: Her Love, the King.

"I cannot live without your love. You have chased after me, broken down my defences, and now I am utterly yours. Kiss me for your love is more delightful to me than the finest wine.

"Let my heart swell to you, my Lord! May the incense of my love for you, brush across your cheek.

"Let Him kiss me with the kisses of his mouth, for your love is more delightful than wine.

"Call me and I will run after you, My Jesus, My love, My closest friend."

"Come away with me, Shula. We must go to my Father's house now."

Shula looked at her Lord. And putting her arm through His, they journeyed together. Her heart was as a feathered thing, testing its wings in her breast.

"May I be lost in you; may I be found in you. Lord, you are my lover, and you are mine and I am yours. That's you, Jesus. I am solely, completely yours."

In the distance we could hear the voices of multitudes all crying out the same theme. "The Bride" the great crowd of witnesses called. "The Bride! She makes herself ready. The groom has built her house!"

Shula smiled. She was finally home.

27

Coming in from the desert region, Shula leaned on Yeshua. I felt so proud. So honoured to be part of that which was long foretold.

"I am your champion," He told her. "I have always been your champion." His words fulfilled all the yearnings of her life. Her heart beat in time with His.

As they walked through the gardens, the flowers chatted to each other, telling of the Glory of God. In the garden, she felt closest to the Lord, giving expression to her heart. Yeshua spent intimate time with Shula. It was there that He taught her to use her weapons given by Him.

"You are powerful beyond measure, Shula. Shine brightly. Love the Lord your God with all you are."

"Let your fire burn in me, Holy One, my Lord, my Jesus," she responded.

The space opened out before her, as she looked through space and time, accompanied by a great shout of worship. Yeshua said, "I cover you in light Shula, my fragrance reaches you."

Taking her by the hand, Yeshua brought her to a bright, white room, infinitely large. Sparkling precious stones were set into the walls. Here, there, living stones were set into the foundations. Light and power vibrated like an orchestra of visual harmony.

It was as tangible as those in the room. The King was here.

"You, Shula, were created as a divine being, to join in the divine council as the image of God. It was always intended to be this way. Long, long ago, I said to the people 'do you not say you are gods? And so you are, created as elohim, for my Father is Elohim. You were never meant to live in a lowly position, but to grow into maturity, to be my counterpart, and to rule with me, and reign with me."

Shula looked at Him, her joy spilling over in her eyes, her face, her hands as they moved to touch Him.

He continued, "You are so beautiful. Your eyes when you look at me, the softness and passion for me are like the eyes of an innocent dove."

His words were as a soft whisper for her ears only, murmuring through the air, driven by the south wind playing with her hair.

"My lover is to me as a cluster of henna blossoms," she told Him.

Shula's Timeline shouted in joy.

He led her deeper into the room, which was lined on both sides with countless Angelic beings.

He spoke in a loud voice, ensuring that all present could hear clearly. "I want to be with you forever. I long for completion. My passion is rising. A mighty rushing wind, flames of fire. I give this to my Father that He may be glorified. He loves having His children around Him."

Yeshua, the Spring of Living Water kept leading Shula forward, toward the towering Holy Presence at the far end of the room. Shula's living letters and her Timeline sang as she walked towards the Lord God. It appeared that her Timeline had been reset, and was back at the beginning, the beginning of creation when all was pure and perfect, every part of it bursting in radiance.

The Angels sang in the most beautiful harmony, cadences flowing over each other like rippling water. It was as though they sang a scented garden to life.

Great is the Lord
He is most worthy of our praise
No one can measure His greatness
Worship the Lord with gladness;
come before Him with joyful songs.

Finally, Yeshua stopped before His Father. Great joy rushed from one to the other. Yeshua presented Shula to His father. "My Lord and my Father. I bring to you the completion of all, for it is done. I bring my Betrothed, that which we have yearned for, longed for, and died for."

The Lord God nodded, tears streaming down His face, for together He and Yeshua, with beautiful Ruach Ha'Kodesh, had battled to bring this about.

"Sing for us," The King said. "Tell us your love," He instructed Shula.

Curtseying deeply, Shula reached into her love and sang forth her joy and promises to Yeshua.

"He comes. He came and found me.
He rides as though to battle - on a white stallion,
Triumphal flag in His right hand.
Love incarnate, the Joy of Joys
You are coming, Jesus
You are coming for your bride
The bride wakens with a mighty shout.
She sees the Bridegroom coming
and makes herself ready.
Together, they ride through the earth,
pushing the forces of darkness back
- further, further.
The triumphant church with her King at her head.
The Song is a prism of colour."

Her voice finished softly, and the Angels caught the last few lines, singing it, multiplying it, enforcing the Kingdom promises.

"She sees the Bridegroom coming
and makes herself ready.
Together, they ride through the earth,
pushing the forces of darkness back
- further, further.
The triumphant church with her King at her head.
The Song is a prism of colour."

Their voices wove and interwove, until the words became reality.

173

God nodded. "My Son," He said, "Sing your bridegroom's song."

"My passion is rising.
A mighty rushing wind, flames of fire.
My splendour is all over you, my Shula,
and we will reign together."

"Bring me Shula's book of life," God commanded.

Angels hurried to the library and carried back books that had SHULA engraved on the covers.

There was such a busyness, as more and more scrolls of life were placed in front of Almighty God.

Every book had SHULA written on the front cover, and under Shula were written other names.

SHULA – *Sharon Nisbet*

Faces flashing past at great speed.

SHULA – *Richard Fellows*

On and on and on.

SHULA – *Ian Johnson*

The Lord's face was wet with tears as He saw His beloved ones' scrolls of life piling high in front of the King.

SHULA – *Susan G O'Marra*

So many books, thousands, millions, uncountable numbers, the names became as one, until everyone whose name was written in the Lamb's book of Life, had SHULA as their name.

SHULA – *Nicolette Morning*

Father God saw every one of them, reading each scroll as they were put in front of Him.

SHULA – *Brandie Muncaster*

Gabriel who was standing behind a table that was groaning under the weight of books, bowed low in worship.

As the Angels worshiped, Ruach Ha'Kodesh flowed over and through the room, taking physical form and settling over the books on the table with a tongue of fire; a fire that burnt but did not destroy.

SHULA – *Toria Newman*

The perfume of the Son enveloped each Angel, tendrils of fragrance winding through the assembly. Whispered words of praise to the Most High God were caught in the rainbow shimmering of Holy Spirit. The whispering grew and multiplied, until ten thousand times ten thousand voices twisted and entwined together as one cry of victory.

Yeshua's presence altered the atmosphere, heightening the love and joy.

He held His hand out to Shula and she stepped forward. She and Yeshua became as one in mystical union. Fused heart to heart, mind of Christ, Spirit Walker, Cloud Dancer.

"Your name is like perfume poured out," the Angels sang.

Shula's Living Letters spelled out the truth of the prophesy on her scroll.

The King smiled, and leaning forward, pressed His signet ring of approval on Shula's book of life, declaring that the finality of all that happened was now done, sealed, approved. "We spoke all this into existence," He said.

Mankind was again clothed in the rainbow garments of Heaven.

As the last of the praise sighed away, the Son, the one on whom all the crowns of earth's realms rested, stood at the table, in the middle of the many books of life.

He laid his hands on the books, tears running down His face and pooling on the scrolls.

"For these, I died. And for these, I live.

APPENDIX

Throughout the book, you will have noticed that Beryl uses the name, **Yeshua**. Whereas Shula uses the name, **Jesus**. These are referring to the same person, the Son of God, God incarnate. Yeshua is the phonetic pronunciation of the Hebrew version, a derivative of the name Yehoshua (Joshua) H3091 (Strong's Concordance), whereas Jesus is the Anglicised version of the Greek Iēsou G2424 (Strong's Concordance).

CHAPTER 1

Across the Sea of Glass: Revelation 4:6 - Across the Sea of Glass that was made from a single precious stone, upon which the rain of the Almighty constantly fell - from G5205 (Strong's Concordance)

Made from a precious stone G2930

Holy Spirit as a female - (1) In the Old Testament, the Spirit of God was always depicted in the feminine. H7307 - rûaḥ - feminine noun. In Torah, the word Shekinah is used which is also a feminine noun. Holy Spirit, Holy Ghost has been referred to in the masculine in Christianity, whereas, we should refer to Holy Spirit in the feminine - consider this: "Let us make mankind in our image, after our likeness" OUR H1823 - dᵊmût is a feminine adverb.

Gen 1:27, "So God created man in His own image, in the image of God, He created him, *male and female* He created them." The image of God is both male and female.

Myrrh - H3874 (Strong's Concordance) to wrap closely or tightly, enwrap, envelop

CHAPTER 6

Spirit of Holiness - feminine noun G42

Romans 1:4; 2 Corinthians 7:1; 1 Thess. 3:13

CHAPTER 7

Spirit of Truth - feminine noun G225 - *alētheia*

John 16:13

CHAPTER 9

Do not the Holy writings say that as Yeshua is now, glorified, so are those who carry His name? 1 John 4:17

Ezekiel 1:28 - rainbow - H7198 Strong's concordance has the same meaning as a bow as in bow and arrow.

CHAPTER 10

The sun is not yellow:

https://www.livescience.com/what-color-sun.html

The throne made of sapphire: Exodus 24:10; Ezekiel 10:1; Ezekiel 1:26

CHAPTER 11

"As I am now, so are they," Yeshua murmured. 1 John 4:17

CHAPTER 15

Sunset and sunrise at the same time can only be seen on the June and December solstices in the Arctic circle. However, the sun rises and then immediately sets.

CHAPTER 17

Constantly behold the face of the Father. Matthew 18:10

for the accuser of our brethren is cast down, which accused them before our God, day and night.

Revelation 12:10

Job 1:7 - 11

CHAPTER 19

I saw her in the foothills of the mountain, where the growth is lush. It was there that Shula became the betrothed, where their chamber was verdant boughs, and beams of cedar, with rafters of firs.
Song of Solomon 1:16, 17

CHAPTER 20

And into her mind came the story Jesus had told of casting pearl before swine. Matthew 7:6

CHAPTER 21

"I agree with your proposal, Lucifer. But be warned! My Betrothed will crush your head."
Genesis 3:15

Forsake not the gathering of yourselves together. Hebrews 10:25

CHAPTER 22

'Nothing, but nothing can separate me from the love of God.' the verse was running through her mind. Romans 8:31

"I will not fear, for what can man do to me?" Psalm 118:6

CHAPTER 23

Come, let us return to the LORD. He has torn us to pieces but he will heal us; he has injured us but he will bind up our wounds. Hosea 6:1

CHAPTER 24

God inhabits the praises of His people. Psalm 22:3

CHAPTER 25

'In everything give thanks, for this is the will of God in Jesus concerning you.' 1 Thessalonians 5:18

Enter His gates with thanksgiving and His courts with praise; give thanks to Him and praise His name. Psalms 100:4

His cheeks are as a bed of spices, as sweet flowers: his lips like lilies, dropping sweet smelling myrrh. His hands are as gold rings set with the beryl: his belly is as bright ivory overlaid with sapphires.
Song of Solomon 5:13,14

Where has your lover gone, most beautiful of women?
Which way did your lover turn?
Song of Solomon 6:1

'Put on the garment of praise for the spirit of heaviness,' Isaiah 61:1-3

'Wait for the LORD; be strong and take heart and wait for the LORD' Psalm 27:14

Song of Solomon 8:8 – 9 and then 10 – 12

Psalm 145:3 'Great is the Lord! He is most worthy of praise! No one can measure his greatness.'

Psalm 100:2 'Worship the Lord with gladness; come before Him with joyful songs.'

CHAPTER 26

Song of Solomon Chapter 4

Ruach Ha'Kodesh: Strongs h7307 Ruach means breath, wind, spirit. When used with Ha'Kodesh (or Qodesh), it means Breath of God, or Spirit of God, Holy Spirit.

CHAPTER 27

I said, "You are gods, sons of the Most High, all of you;" Psalm 82:6

Jesus said, "Is it not written in your law 'I said you are gods'" John 10:34

LIVING LETTERS

SHULA - שולה

ש Sin Numerical value 300, consume

ו Vav 6. secure hook

ל lamed 30   go toward, tongue,

ה Hay 5, to reveal

total: 341

300 = The glory of God

41 = new beginning after testing/trial. Love after trial

THE RAINBOW

The wavelengths of visible light (rainbow) are:

Violet: 380–450 nm (688–789 THz frequency)

Indigo: 420 – 450 nm.

Blue: 450–495 nm.

Green: 495–570 nm.

Yellow: 570–590 nm.

Orange: 590–620 nm.

Red: 620–750 nm (400–484 THz frequency)

ABOUT THE AUTHOR

Jesus is the centre of all that Justine is. She is a revelatory prophetic writer, who is passionate to see the Church in her rightful place in Christ. With a lifetime of knowing the Lord, her inner strength and understanding of the things of God, shows in her daily interactions with others.

Justine and her husband, Stan, live in Auckland, New Zealand, together with their two crazy cats. They have two beautiful adult daughters.

Email: justineorme@justineormeauthor.com
Facebook: www.facebook.com/theauthorjustine
Instagram: www.instagram.com/justineorme

Have you read "In the Beginning - I Am Beryl" Book One (2018)? If not, it's a must-read!

This is the first book in the 5-book chronology taking you through the Biblical accounts from the perspective of the Beryl Stone, mentioned 8 times in the Bible, from before Time to John's Revelation of the end of time.

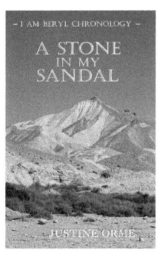

"A Stone in My Sandal – I Am Beryl" Book Two (2019) is the second book in the Chronology of Beryl. This time, we find Beryl among the Israelites in Egypt as he witnesses the transformation of Moses (Moshe) into a leader, and the miracles God performs to free the Israelites from slavery and then teach them who God is, once again. If you thought you knew the story of Moses and the 10 plagues, think again! Justine brings out truths many have overlooked in this historical and Biblical account. Don't miss it!

In "25 to Life" (2019), Justine writes with great power and sensitivity about the very personal and painful subject of child abuse.

Melissa's story is one of hope for all, which allows the reader to see that the only path to lasting freedom in any situation is through Jesus Christ and Him alone.

For 25 hours, we follow James and Melissa as they journey towards Time Weaver, and back to life.

"Arabella – by the sword of the Lord and the word of her testimony" (2021) is a parable of the Christian life, where intimacy with Jesus is an everyday experience. The great awakening of the Sons of God is at the door, and the harvest is ready. Calling all who love the Lord into their Sonship with Father God.

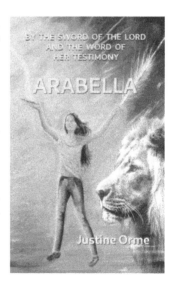

Lightning Source UK Ltd.
Milton Keynes UK
UKHW010134090223
416726UK00007B/81